AFOOT

AFOOT

A Tale of the Great Dakota
Turkey Drive

GEORGE BRANDSBERG

Library of Congress Number: 2004098151

ISBN: Hardcover   0-9771844-0-4 (previously 1-4134-7010-6)
        Softcover   0-9771844-1-2 (previously 1-4134-7011-4)

Photo credits:
George Brandsberg (prairie scene)
Dan Donnert (portrait of author)
WATT Publishing/ Turkey World (turkeys)
Cover design by Bob Holcombe

The Cedartip Company
Manhattan, Kansas 66505-0231
www.cedartip.com

CONTENTS

For Dee, Anne, and Becky
for their patience, love, and laughter
on the trail, looking at every rock
west of the Mississippi.

Chapter 1
ROBBED AT THE END OF THE LINE

"Wanna see 'em dry-dock a riverboat?" Suddenly a big kid was standing beside me, grinning like a monkey. He wore a ragged shirt and frayed work pants held up by one suspender. Right behind him was another fellow in better clothes, but I remember the soles of his shoes flapped when he walked and he wore no socks.

"C'mon! It's really amazing how they can pull a big boat up on dry ground with only a little donkey." He started moving away.

I just shook my head. *No thanks.*

"He's right, you know," the other guy piped up. He was about a foot taller then me, probably two or three years older, too. "You'll probably never get to see that operation again."

By now I knew I should have run for it. I really didn't intend to ask, but I wanted to know. "Why would they haul a steamboat out of the water?"

"Got to fix the leaks. Those ol' boats hit snags and sandbars all the time. When they come into port, they have to fix 'em."

"Let's go. They must be halfway done by now."

I couldn't see any sign of a steamboat being pulled out of the river. They noticed I was looking around and the one named Butch explained, "It's on the other side of that warehouse."

They could see how suspicious I was.

"It's okay, it's okay. Lots of people around. You'll see," the other one, Mike, said impatiently.

So we started walking toward the warehouse. They were hurrying me along, I thought because they were eager to see the dry-docking. As we got nearer the warehouse, it seemed quieter. Unlike the other warehouses where workmen and wagons were coming and going at a frantic pace, there was no one here. But just then, I didn't realize what that meant.

A moment later, we walked briskly around the end of the building. Suddenly, Butch and Mike each took hold of my arms up high and dragged me inside. Swiftly, they jerked off my heavy wool coat and went through its pockets before I could protest.

Almost as quickly, Butch wrapped an arm around my neck and started choking me. Mike stepped toward me and I kicked him as hard as I could in one knee. He yelped with pain, grabbing it for a moment. But in no time, he recovered and went through my pants pockets, emptying them. My eleven dollars! Gone!

Mike pulled a big Barlow knife out of his own pocket,

flipped it open, and waved it under my nose.

"I'm gonna stick 'im, especially for kicking me," he said with a scary laugh. "Right in the guts."

Butch held me tight, even though I tried to wrench free. "Aw, he ain't worth killin'. Let's get outta here!" Butch sounded a little frightened. Maybe he was afraid Mike really would stab me. I was so scared I couldn't say anything, couldn't even breathe.

Next thing I knew, Butch shoved me through a doorway into a dark room so that I landed on my hands and knees. It was tiny, like a closet. Before I had a chance to get up, Butch slammed the door shut. There was a snapping sound, like a latch or a kind of hook that locked me in.

Now I was furious, screaming at the two bullies for robbing me. Their laughter faded quickly as they ran off. My eyes were hot and wet with tears and I choked back a sob. *Thirteen is too old to be a crybaby,* I told myself. But I was mad as could be. Being locked in that dark room scared me, too. *What if I miss my boat?*

What a mess I'm in. Everything I've done since I escaped from Uncle Asa has gone wrong. Lucinda was supposed to be at the Hubbard House Hotel in Sioux City, Iowa. Gone. Got a job at the Germania Hotel in Yankton, Dakota Territory. She was gone when I got there, too. Took a stage coach to Pierre, upriver.

For nearly three days I had ridden trains, crossing half of Illinois and all of Iowa. I had eaten alone. I was careful not to talk to anyone to make sure no one would knew I was Joshua Greene from Kankakee, Illinois.

Though disappointed to the point of tears with the way things were turning out, I found the frontier town of

Yankton fascinating. The streets were bustling with wagons being loaded or unloaded with freight. Carriages, buggies, and people on saddle horses wove their way through the wagons. Indoors, the stores and shops were filled with customers.

Besides a few elegantly dressed gentlemen and ladies in fine silk dresses, there were workmen in homespun, some men in buckskin shirts and pants, and even an occasional Indian decked out in blankets and a mixture of their own garments and those gotten in the settlement. Someone said there was an encampment of Sioux at the edge of town with native goods to trade or sell.

The river front was equally busy. Six steamboats were moored, one unloading stacks of stiff buffalo hides. Workers swarmed over the other vessels, lugging aboard cases of canned or bottled food, machinery, crates of supplies bound for the Indian agencies, the gold camps, and military outposts in the wilderness.

There was so much to see that I know I must have been gawking like a country bumpkin. But, golly, it was *interesting.* It didn't really matter how amazed I looked. I know I must have looked even stranger wearing a big winter coat on a warm September day, but it was easier to keep it on my back than to carry it under my arm. Butch and Mike could have spotted me from a mile away. If I just hadn't let my guard down, I wouldn't have gotten robbed and trapped.

For a while I yelled for help, but no one came. Kicking at the door did no good. It was heavy and thick, letting in only a bit of light around the edges. By ramming it as hard as I could with my shoulder, I found that the crack of an opening got a little wider each time. My shoulder really hurt by the time the hook broke and the door flew open, sprawling me in the dirt of the warehouse floor.

Running, I went back to the spot where I had met the thieves, but, of course, there was no sign of them. Then I looked for a policeman, but couldn't find one in the street. Suddenly, I realized, *I can't go to the police. Suppose Uncle Asa reported my running away to the law? Even though I'm five hundred miles from home, they might be looking for me.*

I felt awful. I had lost my coat. My money was gone. And the thought that the police might be looking for *me* really made me feel low. All of a sudden, the buzzing streets of Yankton were filled with menacing people who wanted to hurt me. A dangerous, frightening place. I just wanted to get out of there. Nervously, I hurried back to the waterfront and sat on the dock until the clerk called passengers aboard the *Key West*.

Somehow I had had the good sense to fold the slip of paper showing I'd paid my passage and tuck it inside the top of one of my socks. All I could afford was fare as a deck passenger—no bed, no private room, not even a hard wooden bench to sit on. But I figured anyone could survive three or four nights outside, especially with the warm Mackinaw coat I had. After booking passage on the riverboat, I had only two five-dollar gold pieces and a silver dollar left.

My valise with my other clothes was safely locked in the luggage room aboard the steamboat, so I hadn't been cleaned out completely. Still, I felt terrible. And really stupid for letting it happen. I found a place along the rail, as far away from anyone as I could get.

Soon, the pilot blew three short blasts with the whistle. A couple of deckhands pulled in the gangplank and cast off the mooring ropes. The boat backed away from the pier and began moving upriver. Now I came around on the right-hand side to watch the shore as we pulled out of Yankton. Soon I spied Mike and Butch on the bank, not thirty feet away.

One of them saw me, pointed directly at me, and started laughing. I was glad that no one else on the boat noticed them.

Chapter 2
COLD NIGHTS ON THE RIVER

The riverboat *Key West* thumped along under two stacks billowing smoke. It was a sternwheeler and from where I was sitting on deck, I could hear the paddles sloshing in the muddy water. I'd heard people talk about the Big Muddy before; now I could see it was a broad stream of tan-colored soup, loaded with fine soil it had carried from hundreds of miles upstream. The movement of water was spooky—swirling and turning so it made small, slurping whirlpools. I wouldn't want to swim in that stuff.

The main channel snaked from side to side, weaving in and out of huge dead trees that had floated down from somewhere and became anchored on the river's sandy bottom in shallow water and some in deep pools, ready to trap any unwary craft, be it a canoe or steamboat.

Sunlight danced on the rippling water, making it sparkle in the gentle breeze. In town, it had seemed hot, making me gasp for breath and sweat from just walking around. But this would have been quite pleasant if my heart hadn't been so heavy.

For the first twelve years of my life, we lived in Kankakee, Illinois, where my parents owned and ran a bakery. Life was grand. Mother and Father rose at three in the morning to make bread, rolls, pies, cakes and wonderful sweet pastries. My sister Lucinda and I would come downstairs at seven o'clock to help. We worked hard, but it was fun. We knew everyone in town and had lots of friends. Father spoke often of building a new house in a nice neighborhood, saying we had lived in the cramped quarters above the bakery for long enough.

In September, 1876, Father and Mother took the morning train to Chicago to buy a new oven to expand the bakery. The next day, a telegram came for us from the Chicago police:

"FIRE DESTROYED BLAKE HOTEL. NO
SURVIVORS. YOUR PARENTS PRESUMED
DEAD."

It had to be a mistake. Lucinda took the telegram out to Uncle Asa's farm—Aunt Clara is Father's sister. He frowned at it and muttered that he'd investigate. The next morning, he took the train to the big city. A day later, he returned and all he did was shake his head "no."

"What about a f-funeral?" Lucinda asked Uncle Asa.

"Funeral? Without bodies? Can't be done." Clearly, the old skinflint, as Father had called him, wanted no part of that.

Stunned, Lucinda and I went through the motions of our old routine. We kept the bakery running, working as always, but with such pain in our hearts that often we couldn't talk.

So when Reverend Smith called on us, we asked again. By now the local newspaper had reprinted articles about the fire from the Chicago dailies and had a notice of the loss of our parents. "We'll have a memorial service next Monday."

Hundreds of people came. Through the tears, I couldn't see who all was there. But I know that Uncle Asa stayed away.

One day in October, Lucinda's dear friend Malcolm stopped to buy doughnuts on his way to work. He was eighteen and had a job as an apprentice bricklayer. We all liked him a lot. He was handsome, funny, and very kind. Lucinda never said so, but you could see how she really liked him.

When Malcolm left the bakery, Uncle Asa was waiting down the street a ways in his rickety old buckboard. He offered Malcolm a ride. That was the end of Malcolm. We never saw him again.

To find out what had happened, Lucinda visited Malcolm's mother, the widow of a railroad worker. Lucinda came home crying pitifully. Malcolm's mother—who had always been nice as pie before—treated my sister like she had leprosy. In icy tones, she said Malcolm had gone to Saint Louis to learn stone masonry.

Uncle Asa must have told an awful lie. I never said anything to Lucinda about seeing Malcolm and our uncle together just before her young man vanished.

On Christmas Day, the old tightwad came to our home and told us it wasn't right for us children to be living on our own, trying to run a business. As a matter of fact, the bakery was doing just fine. But he said he had seen a lawyer and that a judge would make him our guardian and executor of our parents' estate.

"That doesn't sound good," Lucinda said later in a frightened whisper. "I can see now why Father was never close to Uncle Asa. He's such a... such a cold, heartless man."

Until then, I hadn't given it much thought. True, Uncle Asa complained about everything from the weather to the color of his neighbor's barn. Everyone knew how stingy he was, wearing threadbare clothes and living like a pauper, even though he owned one of the largest farms in the county and was actually rich.

Next thing we knew, the Greene Family Bakery was closed; Lucinda was given a job as a housemaid for a wealthy family on Kankakee's sumptuous East Court Street; and I went to the farm with Uncle Asa and Aunt Clara. She was always very quiet and kept to herself. Everything she cooked came out gray and tasted like old boiled potatoes. She never let her bread dough rise enough before baking it. Even I knew better than that.

Uncle Asa was a hog farmer and wore the smell with grim pride. Right off, he had me cutting firewood, fixing fences, hauling wagonloads of grain, husking and shelling ear corn, feeding the hogs, and never sitting down for a minute except to eat. He took me out of school, saying I'd had enough book learnin'. Practically over night, I had become his slave.

One Sunday in March, Lucinda came to visit me on the farm. Uncle Asa never gave us a moment by ourselves, never let us *really* talk to each other. He took her back to

Kankakee in his rattletrap buggy, but as she gave me a hug when we parted, she slipped a note into my coat pocket.

"He's gotten a lawyer and plans to sell our bakery! I'm going to try to stop him, but don't know if I can. Things are *so bad* where I am. I believe you're having a terrible time, too. We must talk soon. Love, Lucinda."

I bet I read that note a hundred times. And each time made me madder. Angrily, I asked, *"How can he do this to us? How can he be so mean?"* We're kin. *How could he do this to members of the family? Well, if he can get a lawyer, we can, too,* I decided. *As soon as I get my chance, I'm going to Kankakee.*

Sure enough, the next Tuesday, Uncle Asa said he would be gone all day, buying a new boar or two. Of course, he wouldn't tell anyone, even Aunt Clara, exactly where he was going. He didn't have enough manners to do that. He sent me to the woodlot to fell small trees and chop them into fence posts six feet long. As soon as he drove his wagon down the lane, I asked Aunt Clara to pack me a lunch. I'd stay in the woodlot all day, I fibbed to her. At a jogtrot, I went to the woodlot, ran through it, crossed a couple fields on neighboring farms, and came out on another road that went to Kankakee, too. It was more than ten miles to town, so walking would take me three hours, anyway.

Luckily, a farmer in a surrey with a spirited team offered me a ride and I was in town in just an hour. I went to the office of Jonathan P. Tibbs, attorney-at-law, where a few months earlier I had delivered sweet rolls every workday morning for the lawyer and his clients to have with their coffee. I had to wait more than an hour before Mr. Tibbs would see me. He had been a friend of my father; I thought he would my friend, too.

"My uncle's stealing everything that belongs to Lucinda and me," I told the elegantly-dressed Mr. Tibbs. "He closed our bakery and is trying to sell it. He ran off Lucinda's beau and he's made me his slave on his pig farm. You got to stop him!"

Mr. Tibbs looked at me for a long time. I could hear his breathing and noticed that his hands were pink and looked as soft as silk pillows. "Does your uncle know you're here?"

"Of course not. He never lets me come to town, never see my friends, never see my sister," I grumbled.

The lawyer shook his head slowly and stared at me for at least two minutes. "There are two things I must say to you: First, your uncle is now your legal guardian. As an adult, he is responsible for your care and your sister's. He is responsible for your parents' estate and can use those assets as he feels appropriate. So, until you're twenty-one years old, you must answer to him.

"Secondly, I am the attorney of record representing Asa Barnes and am not concerned with your problems."

"*But what he's doing is wrong!*" I said desperately.

"Good afternoon, Master Greene. Some day you'll thank your uncle for all his kindnesses." The lawyer got to his feet, signaling that our meeting was over.

A hopeless feeling mashed me. Lucinda and I were stuck with Uncle Asa. He could anything he wanted to with us. Dejected, I left the lawyer's office, trudged all the way back to the farm, and arrived at dusk.

Aunt Clara gave me a plate loaded with a chunk of her bread, covered with lukewarm, gray, lumpy gravy. I tried one bite, nearly choked on it, and went to bed. I couldn't eat anything.

It was very late when Uncle Asa came home. He stormed into my cold attic bedroom, yanked off the quilt and gruffly ordered me to get up and get dressed. I had barely gotten to sleep when he came; I couldn't imagine what he wanted. He said he needed help unloading his new boars.

At the hoghouse, he lunged in the dark, grabbed the front of my coat and gave me a big jerk, pulling me up off my feet. The suddenness of it surprised me, but when he spoke, terror shot down my spine like an icicle.

Uncle Asa was furious. "You sneak off to see a lawyer behind my back?" Before I could answer, he shook me violently and shoved me back against the hog shed. "After all I've done for you, you go and act like this!"

"What have you done for me?" I shouted. "You've ruined my life. My sister's, too!" Now I began to cry.

"You whimpering little snot! I oughta break your neck." This time he slapped my face so hard it stung for a long time. "You say anything about this to Clara and I'll call you a liar." Roughly, he pushed me away and stalked off in the dark. Next thing I heard was his slamming the front door of the house. Only after I quit crying did I go back inside.

In late April, Lucinda ran away. No goodbyes, no notes. She must have been awfully unhappy.

"Good riddance to bad rubbish," said Uncle Asa.

Aunt Clara gave me a sad, helpless look and went back to her kitchen range to cook up some more gray stuff.

She called it dumplings. I couldn't think up a name bad enough for it.

The Fourth of July was the first time I went to Kankakee after my disastrous trip to see Lawyer Tibbs. The year before, 1876, fabulous celebrations around the country had been held on July 4, observing the one-hundredth anniversary of independence. This year was a much tamer commemoration with a short parade and boring speeches in the town square.

To my surprise, Uncle Asa let me do as I pleased. He even gave me a quarter to spend. Tired of listening to the speech making, I walked out of the square and wandered the streets for a while.

Before I knew it, I was walking down Oak Street toward the old Greene Family Bakery. Curiosity pulled me along faster and faster. The last block, I was actually running. What a disappointment! The building was the same, but the sign was gone and a hardware store had moved in. At first, I had an urge to go inside and see who was there now. But I couldn't. A lump grew in my throat and my eyes got watery, thinking about my mom, her wonderful cooking, and how she loved to laugh. I had to think about something else, quick. Spinning around, I wanted to get out of there fast.

"Why, hello, Josh! How are you?" The man was wearing his superb smile, as usual, and extended his hand warmly. It was George Schoolcraft, the postmaster of Kankakee, a faithful customer of the Greene Family Bakery and another regular on my delivery route.

"What do you hear from Lucinda?" he asked.

"Nothing," I said with a shrug.

A puzzled look came over Mr. Schoolcraft's face. "That's odd. I recall seeing letters that she had sent to you. Two or three of them from places in Iowa."

"I never got them," I said. How could that be? Uncle Asa again, that's how!

"Hmm. They must have gotten lost somehow," he said thoughtfully. "Next time there's mail for you, I'll personally hold it at the post office. I take offense at people interfering with the U. S. mail."

"I don't get to town very often anymore."

"Well, when you do, please come and see me," the postmaster said, bidding me farewell and walking away with his family.

On the way back to the farm in the buckboard, I asked Uncle Asa if any mail had ever come from Lucinda. The only answer I got was a little twitch in the back of his neck and silence.

"I wonder *where* she is," Aunt Clara said. "Poor child."

Uncle Asa let out a disapproving snort. I suspected he knew exactly where Lucinda was and wouldn't ever tell anyone else.

The first week of September, 1877, was too rainy to work in the fields. Until then, ol' Uncle Asa had me hoeing corn in the steamy summer heat. One morning, he said he was going to town to have some blacksmith work done and that I could come along. While he was busy talking crops with another farmer, I sneaked off to the post office to see Mr. Schoolcraft.

"This just came yesterday!" he said with a grin, handing me a letter from Lucinda. "And here's one for Lucinda, too. It's from someone in Saint Louis."

I grabbed the two letters and dashed out of the post office.

"You're welcome!" he called after me with amusement.

"Thanks! Thanks!" I yelled back. In seconds, I ripped open the envelope from Lucinda. She was in Sioux City, Iowa, working at the Hubbard House Hotel as a maid. She said she couldn't understand why I hadn't written her. She was well, but worried about me. "Do write me as soon as you can," she said before closing.

Even before I had opened the letter, I knew I was going to Sioux City, Iowa, soon. Reading the short message convinced me all the more that that's where I had to be. Out from under the heavy hand of Uncle Asa and away from his smelly pigs. Lucinda would soon be eighteen and then we could come back, get a lawyer and recover the money Uncle Asa had gotten from selling our bakery.

I had some savings that Father had put in a bank in Kankakee for me, unless Uncle Asa had taken that, too. Lucky for me, it was still there—nearly fifty dollars. That was enough for a train ticket to Sioux City with plenty left over.

Two weeks later, on September 22, Uncle Asa sent me out to mend fences. The night before, I had sneaked my wool Mackinaw coat and valise out of the house and into the haymow of the barn. When I was certain no one would see me, I gathered them up and headed for the woodlot and road beyond. *No more pig-farming slavery for Joshua Greene!* I told myself triumphantly.

* * *

While brooding about not finding Lucinda in Sioux City and being robbed in Yankton, I had fallen asleep. The shrill whistle of the *Key West* woke me as we approached a landing at a tiny place called Bon Homme. It was late afternoon now and my stomach was beginning to rumble. I had eaten a nice meal upon arriving in Yankton, but that was at noon, hours earlier.

But now I had no money. Other deck passengers had brought their own food or went to the steamboat's elegant dining room. I went to the water barrel and took a big drink, but that didn't help much.

A few passengers got off at Bon Homme. The crew loaded firewood and the *Key West* soon got underway again, pushing upriver until it was almost dark. This time it landed at a little Indian agency and tied up for the night. Men had crowded up against the bar at one end of the boat's restaurant cabin. They were smoking, drinking, and talking loudly. Some were sitting at tables, playing cards. A man began playing a piano, too, and as the crowd drank and loosened up, they started singing, louder and louder. The noise went on and on for hours.

All the while, I got hungrier and hungrier until I couldn't think of anything else. To make matters worse, the chill of the September night on the river was especially damp and cold. How I wished I had my wonderful Mackinaw coat now!

Long after midnight, the merrymakers went to their cabins and to bed one by one. By now, I was freezing and starving. At first, I was afraid to go inside. But now, if I didn't, I might not make it through the night. *The worst they can do was to send me back out onto the open deck.*

For courage, I took a deep breath and pushed through the batwing doors into the quiet saloon.

"Ve are closed," the large bartender said with a thick Scandinavian accent. He was standing behind the bar, washing glasses and setting them upside down on a towel to dry.

"Th-that's all right," I said with my teeth chattering from the cold. "I just want to warm up a little."

"Vere's your coat?" he asked me sternly.

"I was robbed. A couple of hooligans in Yankton took it and all of my money."

"Und you're a deck passenger viddout clo'es to keep varm." He shook his head. "Is miserable to be cold viddout no money."

"It sure is." I climbed up on a bar stool to watch him work. Not far away on the bar was a platter with one ham sandwich, some sliced summer sausage, cheese, and pickled pigsfeet on it. Next to the platter was a bowl containing five hard boiled eggs. I guessed this place was like one saloon in Kankakee. It had a sign in the window that said, "Free Lunch." But there was no free lunch. You had to buy a glass of beer or whiskey to get in on the eats. The sandwich and cheese made my mouth water. In fact, I was so hungry I could have eaten even the pickled pigs feet.

"You vant somet'ing to eat?"

I held out my hands in a gesture of helplessness. I had just told him I had no money.

"Go ahead. Eat all you vant. Vat's left over, I t'row out."

I wolfed down the sandwich, a couple of slices of nice, orange cheddar cheese and three of the boiled eggs. All that made my mouth so dry I almost choked. Without saying a word, the bartender put a glass of milk in front of me and nodded. It tasted real fresh and cool.

"What can I do in return to help you?" I asked.

First he shook his head and then, remembering, he said, "*Ja*, you could sweep the floor for me. Dat would be real good."

As we both worked, he told me people called him Ole the Swede, even though he was from Norway. Sometimes he helped cook food for the passengers, but usually he tended bar. He was very tall, broad, and trim and had the bluest eyes I've ever seen.

We both finished our work at the same time. I was about to ask if I could spend the night inside, but he had already guessed what was on my mind. He said all the deck passengers would want to come in then and the captain would yell at him.

"Well, thank you very much for the good food," I said, backing toward the door.

"Tank you very much for the good help. But before you go, take some breakfast and I got somet'ing else for you." He opened a door of a little closet and pulled out an Army blanket. "Sometimes we got U.S. soldiers on dis boat, so we keep extry blankets for them. You take this. Give it back when you get off the boat."

"Are you sure? Won't you get in trouble?"

"Naw, ve're in de territories now. Is okay."

Ole the Swede saved my life on that river voyage and made me feel a lot better about the human race. For the next three nights I helped him clean up after he closed the saloon. He gave me the leftover food. When I returned the blanket the fourth morning, he solemnly shook my hand and wished me well.

Raising his index finger, he declared, "One t'ing more." He took out some coins and handed them to me, saying, "I hate being broke. Even if you have only a few pennies in your pocket, dat's better den nuttin,' especially when you meet up with your sister."

Chapter 3
JOBLESS

Eighty-three cents. The moment I got off the steamboat, I counted it. Two quarters, a dime, four nickels, and three pennies is what Ole the Swede paid me for helping him on the *Key West.* It was a lot, considering all the food he had given me, too.

The landing at Fort Pierre was a small, flat area with a few sheds for storing cargo from the river steamers, awaiting transshipment by freight wagon. The village of Fort Pierre was a motley collection of log cabins, sod huts, and shanties hastily nailed together next to the fallen-down trading stockade that gave the settlement its name. It was a rough place filled with hard men and a few women that looked even tougher.

But knowing that I would soon see Lucinda in Pierre, across the river, cheered me. To get there would require taking one of the small flatboat ferries between the two settlements. The one-way fare for a single passenger was a dime. I didn't want to part with any of my coins, so I looked for a way to cross without paying.

Among the wagons loading freight was a small one onto which a thin old man by himself was loading trunks and suitcases taken off the *Key West*. He was panting and red in the face, working as fast as he could, which was slow.

"Is that load bound for Pierre?" I asked him.

"Sure is."

"Can I help you load up for the price of the ferry ride?"

"Sure, if you do your share."

I swung my valise into the wagon box and boosted up suitcases, hat boxes, a few small wooden crates, and burlap sacks of hardware. The larger trunks we lifted up together, one of us on each end. It was hard work, but didn't take very long. When I tried to chat with the drayman, he wouldn't talk, even after we climbed up onto the seat and started for the ferry landing.

An hour later, we drove up the muddy street to the Grand Central Hotel in Pierre. I tossed off my valise and hopped down, ready to run inside to find Lucinda. Since she had worked in a hotel in Sioux City, I figured she'd be working in this hotel now.

"Where do you think *you're* going?" the driver growled at me.

"I got business to attend to."

"Your business is to help me unload this wagon!"

That wasn't what I had agreed to, but we really hadn't discussed any details. The poor man did need help and it would take only a few minutes, anyway, so I stayed. When we were through, I grabbed my heavy valise and hauled it inside the hotel.

"I'm looking for my sister, Lucinda Greene," I told the hotel desk clerk with a big smile on my face.

"Is she a guest?"

"I don't know. More likely she's a maid or laundress at this hotel."

"We don't have any Lucindas working here."

"Where are the other hotels in town?"

"Ain't any," he said with a shrug. "Well, there's a boarding house down on the waterfront. But that's no place for a lady."

I didn't like what I was hearing. I expected Lucinda to be right there to greet me. It was plain to see that this man couldn't care less that she wasn't there. *Why isn't she here?* I wanted to scream at the top of my lungs. "She's *got* to be here," I insisted.

"She ain't," the clerk said, pleased to see me upset.

"I mean she has to be somewhere here in Pierre. Would you keep my valise until I find her?"

He dinged a little bell to summon a young man who took my bag to a luggage room. *No other hotels. Maybe she found a job in a restaurant. Or a bakery. She's got to be working in some business here. Or maybe in someone's home. Finding her will take some time.*

At two different restaurants I visited, the reply was the same: "Never heard of her."

The lady in a millinery shop said she thought she had talked to someone by that name, a young woman looking for work.

"A pretty girl with long, brown hair, about this tall?" I

asked, reaching above my head.

"Mmm—"

"From Kankakee, Illinois!"

"Why, yes, I do recall she mentioned Illinois." But that's all the woman could remember.

The rest of the morning I spent going up and down the street, stopping in businesses, asking about Lucinda. No one else knew anything about her. By now I was so desperate that I tried a feed store, a livery barn and even a dentist's office. On the way back to the hotel, I passed a bakery that was closed. Even there, I stopped and banged on the front door, but no one answered.

Where are you, Lucinda? What's happened to you? I was mad at her for not being right there, but the anger was giving way to worry. *Suppose something's happened to her—that she was kidnaped and someone has her locked up in a shack in this dismal town! Or maybe she's gone back to Yankton. Or Sioux City! Or even Kankakee!*

Oh, Lucinda, how could you do this to me? Now I was really upset. I don't know whether I was more angry about not finding her or more worried that she had met some horrible fate. *Why, some riverboat roosters or even the Indians might have her!*

Back at the hotel I calmed down. I ate a lunch of soup, crackers and a piece of apple pie for ten cents. The more I thought about it, the more I knew I shouldn't blame Lucinda. She couldn't know that I had run away from Uncle Asa's pig farm or that I was looking for her. But her moving from one town to another had cost me all my money and had put me in a scary predicament.

What if I can't find her? That frightening thought had

occurred to me before, especially during my low-spirited time on the riverboat. This was a nightmare that was coming true.

All afternoon, I visited the business places I had not been to in the morning, even the saloons and the boarding house along the waterfront. Everywhere I went, I got the same discouraging response: "Lucinda who? Nope, never heard of her."

Seventy-three cents. Better make it last as long as I can. For supper I had a sandwich and a glass of milk for a dime. *Sixty-three cents.*

Not knowing what else to do, I went and sat in the lobby of the hotel, pretending to wait for Lucinda. A different clerk was at the desk now. If he asked, I had already decided to tell him I was waiting for my sister to meet me. In the middle of the night, he woke me up.

"Still waiting?"

"Unh—yeah. I thought she would be here by now."

"What's her name?"

"Lucinda Greene. With an 'e' at the end."

"Hmm." For a moment, he was thinking real hard. "There's something about that name—"

I told him all about her.

"Just a minute." He walked over to the counter, leafed through the guest register, and said, "Here it is! She was a guest here for two nights—September 9 and 10. She has long hair, light brown. I remember she's a pretty girl."

"Yes!"

"Is she expecting you? Do you want a room for the night?"

"No, thanks. She'll be here soon. I'm fine here."

"There's a wash room at the end of that hall. I'll send down a pitcher of warm water."

After cleaning up, I spent the rest of the night in that large overstuffed chair, getting little sleep. By morning, I decided I had to find a job to tide me over till Lucinda came.

The morning was real discouraging. Everywhere I asked for work I was told they didn't need anyone or that I was too young, too small, or too inexperienced. And of course, no one had ever heard of Lucinda Greene. For lunch I had a piece of apple pie and a glass of milk. They charged me fifteen cents, which was highway robbery! *Forty-eight cents. Soon I'll be broke and starving.*

Because there was nowhere else to ask, I stopped at a blacksmith shop. I stood around for a long time before one of them interrupted his work to talk to me. Of course, he had no work for me and hadn't seen Lucinda. I asked him why the bakery on main street was closed.

"The owner's been sick. He's probably broke. His wife left him, too." He wiped his hands on his leather apron, glanced at the sun to see what time it was and said he had to go. Instantly, he was hammering a piece of iron, taken red-hot from the forge.

A man in a dry goods store two doors down from the closed bakery told me the owner was Jim Langley. He and his wife had come from Pennsylvania and opened their bakery a year ago and did well until Mr. Langley began having strange pains. Gradually, he couldn't even get out of bed. For a while his wife tried to run the business by herself, but it was too much for her. Hoping to make a new start, she shipped some of their baking equipment to the Black Hills.

"Seems she had a new partner, too, a young woman. You'd have to ask Jim about that."

Mr. Langley was under the care of a doctor and was staying at the boarding house near the waterfront, where someone could bring him his food and look after him. On the way to the boarding house, I was almost afraid to visit the ailing man. If he knew anything about Lucinda— where she was, what she was doing, how she'd been—he would probably tell me she had gone off somewhere else again.

"Yes! Lucinda Greene is her name," the sick man said with a wheeze. "When I'm better, I'm going to join them in Deadwood. I'm expecting a letter from them any day now."

My heart sank into my socks. I wanted to cry. *How can she be gone again?* And me with just pennies left, no job, no prospects.

"You're sure?" I asked, hoping it wouldn't be true.

"They left two weeks ago with a big stove, ovens, a thousand pounds of flour, four hundred pounds of sugar, and everything else to open a good bakery."

I tried to hide my disappointment, but I couldn't. For years I had greatly admired my sister, Lucinda. She was smart, friendly, and pretty. But this was crazy. To get to Deadwood, she had to cross more than two hundred miles of dangerous Indian territory and when she got there, she would be in a rowdy, lawless, horrible place. The stories I had heard about Deadwood on the *Key West* chilled me. Robberies, murders, scalpings. And Lucinda, bless her innocence, must have lost her mind to actually go there.

After leaving Mr. Langley's dingy room, I wandered up the main street of Pierre. Behind the blacksmith shop was a wagon yard where freight from back east was loaded onto wagons bound for the Black Hills. Maybe I could get a job on a wagon train to Deadwood.

"*You* a mule skinner? Haw, haw, haw!" replied the first man I asked. He and his friends were all large, coarse men who talked in loud voices and laughed at everything, funny or not.

After four tries, I talked to a man who was totally different. He wore a dark gray suit and derby hat. His hands were knobby and callused from hard work, but they were clean. "What can you do?"

"I can drive a team of horses or mules. I can ride. I can cook. I can load and unload wagons."

"You're on the light side for handling freight. You look more like a cook's helper to me. How old are you?"

"Fourteen—almost."

"That's young. In a week or so, we'll have a train leaving Fort Pierre for Deadwood. If you're still looking for work by then, come and see me at Volin Brothers Warehouse across the river."

"Thanks a lot."

At the far end of the yard, a group of teamsters were playing cards. Two men were perched on the tongue of a wagon, the others sat on the ground in a semi-circle. In the middle there was a pile of money, more than a hundred dollars.

To see better, I climbed up into the wagon and leaned into the near corner of the box. For maybe fifteen minutes,

I watched and soon got really disgusted with their crude talk. *When they finish playing this hand, I'm leaving.*

Crack! The noise made me jump a foot in the air. I thought someone had fired a pistol right at me. Nearly twenty feet away stood a grimy giant, laughing like a donkey.

"Hey, Rufus, leave the greenhorn alone."

"Get out of my wagon, you little snot." To that he added a bunch of words I will never repeat.

I scrambled down. Now all of the men were laughing at me.

The man with the bull whip waddled up to me, gave me a little shove and growled, "Better run home to mommy, little boy."

He was the ugliest man I had ever seen. He was huge, much bigger than Ole the Swede. But this man was filthy. His clothes looked like they had never been washed. The collar and cuffs of his heavy shirt were crusted with grease. Tousled brown hair protruded from under his battered felt hat, his eyes were bloodshot, and his belly hung over his wide leather belt like a sack of lard, hiding the top of his baggy pants. The lower half of his face was darkened by a grizzly stubble and the corners of his mouth were stained with tobacco juice. He was really disgusting.

"*Well, you goin?* This ain't no playground for no children."

I turned around and started to walk away. When I'd gone a few feet, the crack of his whip exploded just behind the heel of my left shoe. But this time, I was expecting it and didn't jump as high as I had earlier. I just kept walking.

The teamsters all laughed loudly again.

"Goodbye, little sissy," Rufus said in a squeaky voice.

Discouraged, I trudged back to the hotel. Now that I knew for certain that Lucinda wasn't coming for me, I had misgivings about sitting around the hotel for another night. I had looked everywhere, including Fort Pierre, for a job with no hope.

Supper cost me two nickels. *Thirty-eight cents left.*

"Is there some work I could do to earn the use of a room for the night?" I asked the clerk. "I don't think my sister will be here tonight."

"How about sweeping and mopping the corridor upstairs? Do that and you can have the little room at the end of the hall. It has just a cot, but it's not too bad."

The work took me an hour. For more than a week I had not slept in a bed, so it was a delight to clean up, crawl into my night shirt and sleep like a rock.

In the morning, I was starving hungry. I ordered eggs, bacon and pancakes for twenty cents. I didn't want to part with that much money, but I *had* to eat. After settling up, I would have eighteen cents left. A dime, a nickel, and three pennies. Before, money had never mattered much to me. Now it was almost the only thing I could think about. I counted the coins several times before slipping them into my pocket.

"Are you looking for a job?" the clerk asked when I paid for breakfast. "A Mr. Peach is looking for drovers to take a herd to the Black Hills."

"Where can I find him?" I asked eagerly.

"Down at the boarding house. He's a big fellow."

When I got there, they told me Mr. Peach was in the

saloon next door. I found him at a corner table, drinking a big glass of whiskey for breakfast. When my eyes adjusted to the darkness of the room, I could see Mr. Peach was the same Rufus who had ordered me off his wagon yesterday.

"What do you want, runt?"

"They say you're looking for drovers."

"Ever work with livestock?"

"Yessir. Horses. Mules and pigs."

"Pigs, huh?" An ugly smirk came across his face, but he didn't say what was on his mind. "If I can get enough *men*, we'll leave tomorrow."

When I asked about the job, he said he'd pay a dollar a day, grub and bedroll provided. The trip would take forty-five to fifty days and it could be risky.

"Got a horse?" he asked.

"Nossir."

"Well, I hope you got good shoes then."

"I do."

He said to be at the Fort Pierre wagon yard at sunrise the next morning, ready to travel. I told him I needed a day's wages in advance. Without hesitation, he handed me the money, but snarled that if I didn't show up, he'd catch me and give me a real hiding.

Clutching the silver dollar, I ran out of the saloon and back to the boarding house to tell Mr. Langley my plans. The clerk told me the sick man was asleep, so before I left, I wrote a little note for him: "I'm going to the Black Hills.—Joshua Greene."

Chapter 4

STARTING OUT

The excitement of leaving on the trail drive kept me awake most of the night. The sky was just beginning to lighten when the screech of a riverboat whistle woke me wide-eyed. Quickly, I packed my valise and checked the room to make sure I had everything.

The sun was just peeping over the bluff behind Pierre as I crossed the river on the ferry. Wisps of fog curled up off the silent Missouri, its water purling and roiling menacingly. Patches of fog hid some points along the shore.

When I got to the wagon yard, I was afraid I'd be scolded for being late; as it turned out, I was the first one there after Rufus Peach. He was perched up on the seat of a big freight wagon, hitched to twelve huge oxen. Fastened to the back of the big wagon was a smaller one. Both carried full loads, hidden under heavy canvas covers to keep them dry. Rufus greeted me with a sour look and continued to pick his teeth with a wooden matchstick he had sharpened on one end for that purpose.

"Where are the cattle?" I asked.

"Just hold on," he grumbled.

Four mounted men rode up. They all wore big felt hats, pistols and pointy-toe boots and rode handsome, powerful-looking horses. I guessed they were cowboys from Texas.

Soon, three more men rode into the wagon yard, carrying small bundles behind their saddles. One was on a black mule, another on a donkey, and the third on a sickly spotted horse, brown and white.

A couple of minutes later, the men present began muttering when an old man in a buckskin shirt, fur hat, and Indian leggings rode up—an old trapper. He was leading a pack horse with a light load. Beside him were two young Indian men, both looking proud.

"I ain't ridin' with no redskins," one cowboy grumbled.

"Maybe they're scouts," one of his companions ventured.

Last to arrive was a frail, wan man wearing a kepi and blue coat of a cavalry officer He had a blank look on his face and eyes that stared straight ahead. But he rode as stiff and proud as I've ever seen anyone do.

"You all make a pretty sorry looking crew," Rufus said, stopping to spit. "Our herd is being unloaded from the steamboat *Nelly Peck* and in a while, we'll push them out of town. If you don't like the looks of this crew, get out now. Once we start, there'll be no quittin' on the trail."

"You ever drive 'stock before," the oldest cowboy asked with a slow, sarcastic drawl.

Rufus replied with a blast of profanity that would have

scorched the paint off a pump handle.

The Texan smiled. "You must hale from the glorious state of Missouri. I jus' hope you can handle a herd as well as you cuss."

Rufus asked how many had firearms. Everyone had a pistol, a rifle, or shotgun, except for me. The cowboys were the only ones whose guns you could see. The burly boss then asked for a show of hands of those who thought they were good shots. Only the old trapper and his young Indian companions replied.

After a while, Rufus ordered the old soldier on the gray mule—his name was Bill—to start driving the wagons up the Black Hills road and wait at the edge of town for the herd to catch up. Then he barked at the rest of us to head for the riverbank.

Three steamers were tied up and all were buzzing with laborers frantically unloading cargo. I couldn't see any cattle. Several horses were being led off one boat. Beyond it was a low fence with something alive and dark inside— maybe goats or hogs.

Rufus strode out in front of us toward that pen. He and I were the only ones on foot; everyone else was still mounted.

One of the cowboys started laughing. Soon the others were hooting and slapping their sides, howling with laughter.

"What's so funny?" Rufus demanded, adding a torrent of blue words.

"You don't expect us to drive *them* to the Black Hills," the oldest cowhand said.

"That's what I hired you for."

"Nossir!" he said indignantly. The good humor had gone out of him like the air in a popped balloon. He turned to his companions and shouted angrily, "C'mon, men, let's get outta here."

By now I had caught up and saw what was in the pen. Turkeys! Hundreds of them were crowded together, looking ruffled and cranky.

"Just wait a dadburned minute, you gawldurned drovers," Rufus roared. "Stick in here with me today at least."

"Forget it!" The lead cowboy was reining his horse away.

"Triple wages for the day!" Rufus yelled.

The oldest cowhand rode off, but his younger riders stayed. Rufus ordered me to open the gate and drive the birds out. When I went inside, the turkeys just stared at me and wouldn't budge when I slapped my hands against my pantlegs and shouted at them. Suddenly, the flock rushed for the gate. Some of the birds began flapping their wings and flying over others in front of them. Just outside the gate, they scattered in every direction.

Oh, Lord, what have I gotten into here? The riders dashed off after the bunches of turkeys and managed to bring them back into a couple of larger groups. Other workmen from along docks joined the fray long enough to move the birds through the small settlement.

It took us almost two hours to catch up with the wagons beyond the village. At that point, the three cowboys demanded their pay, accepted it, and rode off, still laughing.

Rufus changed places with the driver of the wagon, popped his whip over the ears of the bulls and got them started at their slow, lumbering pace. The rest of us stationed ourselves at the sides and rear of the flock and by hollering and waving our arms, made the birds follow the wagon. Once in a while a turkey would dart after a grasshopper or other insect, pulling bunches of other birds out of the flock with it. Our riders quickly circled the wanderers and turned them back into the herd. We followed the road up a small valley and onto the bare plains beyond the Missouri breaks.

I was the only person who had to walk. When turkeys near me strayed, I had to run as fast as I could to get around them and chase them back into the herd.

At midmorning, Rufus halted the wagon beside a small creek, unhitched the bulls and turned them loose to drink and graze for a while. He told us to let the turkeys spread out so they could forage for food, but be careful they didn't scatter too far.

He yelled, "Hey, you!" at me and said I would be the cook. "Make coffee and rustle up some grub. Everything is in the small wagon."

All I could find was a sack of salt pork, some large tins of soda crackers and two wooden barrels of drinking water. It was embarrassing not to be able to find the supplies. Already, I knew that if I asked Rufus where everything was, he'd bawl me out.

"Well, get on with it!" he bellowed when he saw I wasn't making any progress.

"I can't find the coffee or coffee pot," I said quietly.

"*What?*" Quickly, he waddled up, threw back the canvas cover on the wagon. "Look up there!" he barked.

Sure enough, there was the coffee pot, a Dutch oven,

three big cast iron skillets and even a little stove, but there was no other food to be found in the wagon.

When I pointed that out, he was furious and let out a stream of foul words, cursing the crew that had loaded the wagon.

"That boneheaded trader left out my order of vittles!" he muttered. "I ought to go back and bust out his rotten teeth."

"What's missing?" I asked.

"The beans and coffee, is all."

"No salt or pepper? How about some rice? Canned goods, like tomatoes and peaches? Some eggs and bacon? Flour for biscuits and gravy? How about corn meal for corn meal bread and mush? Some sugar and molasses and so on?"

"We ain't runnin' no restaurant here," he growled.

"That's for sure," I said. "But we need more supplies."

"Then make a list and I'll send Bill and the old coot back to get stuff," he thundered, cussing fiercely.

A half-hour later, creepy old Bill and the ancient trapper, Zebulon something, rode off, returning to Fort Pierre. Zeb's Indian companions wanted to go with him, but Rufus made a big fuss about being short-handed and the old trapper persuaded them to stay with us.

For two hours we sat around after having a little water and soda crackers for lunch. I had made a big list that included apples, cheese, dried fruit, summer sausage, some cuts of fresh beef and pork, but Rufus crossed off a lot of things before handing it to Bill. It amazed me that the boss of this drive hadn't even made sure we had food. What else had he missed?

As we pushed the herd up the trail again, a train of mule-drawn wagons passed us from behind. Later in the day, we met a long string of wagons coming from the mountains. Everyone who saw us pointed at us and laughed. At first, I thought driving turkeys was amusing, but the novelty soon wore off.

An hour or so later, some horsemen rode up from the west, and seeing our flock, began firing their pistols in the air. The frightened turkeys flew and scampered away from the loud shots. To the riders, that was hilarious.

Rufus dowsed their good humor by using his bullwhip to pop the rear-end of one horse. The animal bolted, spilling the man from the saddle. The victim scrambled to his feet, looking like he would attack Rufus, but thought better of it and stood in place, glaring at the wagon boss.

One of his companions retrieved the runaway mount and they all moved on. It took us nearly an hour to get the flock moving up the road again.

The prospect of spending the night with a flock of turkeys worried me. How could we possibly keep those mindless birds together in the dark? I hoped Rufus Peach had a plan for that. As it turned out, he did. Among the supplies in the smaller wagon were several rolls of woven wire fence and steel posts to make a pen about four feet high and one hundred feet across. As long as the turkeys stayed calm, that would work. But if they got stirred up or if something plunged them into a panic, they could easily fly over that fence.

At mid-afternoon, we turned off the road and went down into a wooded valley before halting to let the bulls and birds forage for feed while we set up the big wire pen.

Toward sunset, we herded the turkeys inside the enclosure. Zeb and Bill were expected back soon with the kitchen supplies. I don't know how they could find us since we had left the main track.

Rufus ordered me to scare up firewood. I asked the other men to help, but they acted like they didn't hear me. The two Indians followed me on their horses and watched me cut dry branches off trees. I was mighty careful to stay within sight of the camp and tried to make sure they never got between me and the wagons.

I kept wondering, *If they scalp me, will they take off all the skin with hair on it or just a strip of skin down the middle of my head? What will my scalp look like dried and hung up? Would they scalp me while I'm still alive? Or kill me first? Would the scalping kill me?* These gruesome thoughts drove spikes of terror into my body and mind and made me shake terribly.

I had the axe in my hands. *Maybe I can fight them off for a short while, but they are bigger and older than me.* Still, after ten minutes or so, they never came any closer and I calmed down some. But I was still shaking with fear. *Oh, Lucinda, I hope I see you again.*

After a half-hour, I had a big pile of limbs. I called to them to help me, but they feigned not hearing. Maybe they didn't understand what I was saying. At any rate, they wouldn't drag any of the fuel back to camp. They laughed softly, probably at me, but didn't lift a finger to help, even after I repeated my request several times.

I had to make seven trips to drag all the branches and other pieces of wood into camp. It was nearly dark when I finished.

Chapter 5
NIGHT RAID

The campfire was crackling nicely when Zebulon and Bill rode in. They unloaded the pack horse and stacked the foodstuffs within the circle of light of the fire. When done, they led their mounts away and turned them loose to graze.

"Get us some grub as quick as you can," Rufus ordered.

I had no idea what he expected, but started by putting water and coffee in the coffee pot and setting it on to heat. I had built the fire between two rows of big rocks set up to hold the iron grate I found in the smaller wagon. The fastest thing to make that I could think of was to fry some potatoes and salt pork and serve tomatoes cold from the can.

Already, the men were grumbling about being hungry and tired of waiting. But do you think they'd offer to help me? Now I remembered when my sister Lucinda or Mother had asked me to peel potatoes or wash dishes and I was always "too busy."

Before long, I had three skillets sizzling over the fire, two filled with sliced potatoes, the third full of salt pork. Zeb rummaged around in the smaller wagon and found tin cups and plates for serving the food. He found only spoons—no forks or table knives. But we were all so hungry that no one cared.

Almost as soon as it was cooked, the food disappeared from the skillets. My plate was the last one filled and none too full at that. *Maybe I should make more*, I thought, but Rufus shot me a scowl that told me that's all we needed that night.

"You sure took plenty for yourself," Rufus growled at me. For a moment, anger flashed inside me and I nearly talked back to him. Luckily, I held my tongue. Later I'd learn how dangerous that was.

For a short time, the entire crew sat around the fire, wolfing down food. Soon, they rose, one by one, dropped their plates and tin cups in a pile by the fire and slank off into the dark.

When I started washing the dishes in a large pan of water I had heated for that purpose, I thought I was all alone. Silently, Zeb appeared beside me with a dishtowel in his hand.

"Been many years since I did this," he said with a little chuckle. "Figured you'd like some help."

No doubt he had seen the frown on my face, even by firelight. I was so tired I could hardly stay on my feet, but there was still so much work to do. I thanked him for his thoughtfulness.

"Might as well make a party of it," he said. Then he uttered a few strange words. Almost instantly, his young Indian friends appeared next to us. He handed each of them a dish towel. "This is my grandson, John Blood. And his friend Eagle Screams. We're all Mountain Crow."

"Mountain Crow?"

"Yes, the mountain band of the Children of the Big Beaked Bird. Long time ago some Frenchies started calling us Crows."

"You're no Indian," I said, disputing his words. True, his face and hands were a deep bronze, but when he rolled up his sleeves or took off his moccasins, he was as white as milk underneath. But his long, gray hair was in braids that draped like ropes in front of his shoulders. His beard was crudely trimmed, a half-inch long.

"Been a Crow more than thirty years," he replied. "I'm more Crow than white and proud of it."

"But the Indians are savages," I protested.

"Watch your mouth when you don't know what you're talking about." The old man's tone had taken a hard edge.

"Do they speak English?" I nodded in their direction.

"John Blood does a bit. Eagle ain't learnt none yet."

"John Blood?"

"One of his fathers—an uncle, actually—named him Blood on His Feet for an act of bravery. As a young brave, the uncle was ambushed by five Paiute warriors. They were all hacking away at each other with knives and the uncle saw his own feet were covered with blood. He says to himself, 'I'm already killed! But these Paiutes will die with me' and his heart was so strong he finished them all. Then he realized the blood on his feet wasn't his at all, but theirs instead. Because John Blood has white blood from me and his father, he wanted his name to be part-white, too. So he became John Blood."

At the sound of his name, the young man leaned forward with a very serious look. "How do?" he asked, offering his hand.

I squeezed it quickly and let go. Something in John Blood's eyes really frightened me. At first I thought it was pure hatred for me, so powerful it made me turn away. Later, I guessed that he was testing me to see if he could scare me. He did it handsomely. I judged him to be three or four years older than myself—seventeen at most—and a full foot taller.

Eagle Screams put out his hand and I shook it, too. There was a warmth in his eyes, a glint of good humor that made me feel better. I wished I could talk to him. "Where's your home?"

Eagle continued smiling at me as though he didn't hear me.

"We come from the Big Horn Mountains in Montana Territory," Zebulon replied.

"Why did you leave?"

"I wanted to show these young hosses something of the white man's world while I could. We rode down the eastern front of the Rockies to Old Taos, crossed the Indian Territories and rode on east to Saint Louie. Then back up the Missouri to the old homeland of the Hidatsa in northern Dakota. We was goin' home from there, but got a chance to ride a steamer down to Fort Pierre. This drive looked like a way for these boys to spend time in a white man camp."

I didn't understand where all they had been, but it sounded like a long journey.

"How did they like the cities?"

"Saint Louie was too noisy. In Omaha, a drunk tried to shoot us. Over all, the cities made a bad impression on these young men."

By now we had finished washing the dishes and pans. Zeb spoke a few words in the Crow language and then he said they'd camp at a little distance from the rest of us.

Rufus waddled up and poured the last of the coffee into his cup. "Old goat sure do like talkin' don't he?"

"He's had an interesting life, I'd say."

"Don't believe him. Anyone who'd take up with the redskins ain't got the sense of a cold rock." Rufus fished a bottle of whiskey out of this coat pocket, poured a dollop into his coffee, and went back to the big wagon where he apparently had a bed roll.

Since no one else was around, I went to the smaller wagon, found a blanket and a canvas tarpaulin and rolled up near the fire. Soon I was toasty warm and drifted off to sleep. Later, I woke up cold. Then the coyotes began yipping and howling, some close, some far away. Their sounds were coming from everywhere and I was sure there were hundreds of them out there, skulking in the dark.

John Blood. Blood on His Feet.

Warriors slashing away at each other with crimson-stained knives. Those probably aren't coyotes out there at all, but Indians making coyote-like calls to signal each other as they sneak up on our camp. For comfort, I crawled into my bedroll and pulled the covers over my head. No sooner had I done that than I had the terrifying thought of being trapped in my bed so that an attacker could smash my skull with a stone axe or thrust a knife into my back. Wildly, I threw off the covers and looked around. My heart was pounding fiercely. *Why did I ever leave Kankakee?*

I wanted to get up and walk about the camp to make sure all was well. But I was afraid to move. *Someone might be out there, just waiting for me to do something stupid like that.* Now my teeth were chattering, but it wasn't from the cold. From time to time, I slipped out of my blanket long enough to put more wood on the fire, fearing that every move I made would be my last. After a while, overwhelming fatigue pulled me down, down to sleep.

Sounds of turkeys gobbling in the dark awakened me. By now the fire had burned down to embers. Something was attacking the birds. I couldn't see anything. But I could hear the whir of their wings and squawks of alarm.

Jumping out of my bedroll, I ran to the big wagon to wake Rufus. I called and called and got only snoring for an answer. Apparently he had drunk so much whiskey before falling asleep that nothing would wake him. Soon, the ruckus with the turkeys stopped. Even the coyotes quit howling. An owl hooted in a tree nearby.

Well, if no one else cares, why should I worry about those fool birds? For a moment I considered building up the fire again, but decided to save the wood for cooking in the morning. Yawning, I rolled up inside the blanket and tarp again and went back to sleep.

A sharp pain came from my backside, jarring me part way out of a deep sleep. Rufus kicked me with the toe of his boot a couple more times before I realized that this was his rude wake-up call.

"Get up, you hare-brained runt! The herd is gone!"

Sitting up, I could see in the dim light of dusk that most of the wire pen had been knocked down during the night. Sure enough, there were no turkeys inside, except for three dead ones with their soft bellies ripped open, apparently by coyotes.

His shirttail hanging out and with only one boot on, Rufus ran lopsidedly to the pen, cursing as he went. He was furious.

The other men appeared, wanting to know what had happened. Zeb, John Blood and Eagle Screams were last to arrive. Eagle had a huge grin on his face. I wished he'd quit because if Rufus saw him smiling, the boss would certainly give him a clout.

Eagle pointed up into the trees. All of them around the flattened pen were filled with the big black birds. At the sounds of danger, they had flown into the trees to roost, safe from the marauding coyotes. Luckily, Rufus saw the turkeys in the trees before he saw Eagle's smile.

"Who was on watch?" Rufus roared.

At first, no one dared answer.

"Nobody stood watch," Zeb said quietly. "You never gave the word."

"That's absolutely stupid!" The boss launched another torrent of profanity, dressing us all down like a dull team of oxen. I don't know about the others, but Rufus's blaming us for his mistake was terribly unfair. He said it was absolutely stupid. It was too bad he couldn't see that it was all his own fault.

Zeb suggested that putting out some feed would bring the turkeys down from their roosts and then we could drive them when ready. John Blood and Eagle Screams stoked up the fire while I made dough for biscuits and got the coffee started.

When the sun came up, I realized I had survived my first night on the trail. The biscuits turned out just fine, but the sausage gravy was on the salty side. *Maybe—just maybe—I'll see Lucinda again.*

Chapter 6

LAYING OVER IN THE RAIN

The next day, the weather was dark and gloomy. Just before noon, a fine misty rain began to fall and gradually turned into a steady drizzle. Within a couple of hours, we were all soaking wet and cold. Rufus spotted a grove of cottonwoods in a low area a quarter-mile off the road and turned the wagons in their direction.

"We've got to get these turkeys to roost tonight so they don't start getting sick," he said, talking more to himself than anyone else on the crew. He told us to scatter some grain around to feed the birds and they ate eagerly. Late in the afternoon, a couple of hens flew up into one of the cottonwoods. By dark, all of them had taken refuge "high and dry" in the trees, as Rufus put it.

The next morning, Rufus was in the worst mood ever, cursing the weather, his luck, and the sorry bunch of people he had hired for the drive. Eying the pouring rain from under his drooping hat, he announced the drive would lay over for the day. He instructed the rest of us to take care of the turkeys, to feed them amply "when they come down from their roost." Then Rufus went back to bed.

Zeb, John Blood, and Eagle found a large tarpaulin and wooden poles in the small wagon, along with some rope. Before long, they had turned the tarp into a shelter that resembled the roof of a tent. Except for Rufus, all the men stood under the tarp, staring at the rain in brooding silence.

The turkeys came down from their perches in the trees and stood around, waiting for something to eat. Their feathers were all wet and drooping. Rain pelted down on them steadily, but they seemed to endure the bad weather remarkably well. After being fed corn, some of them browsed in the grass, apparently finding more to eat. Later, they stood around in small bunches, eyeing us under our tent-like shelter with what I suspected was a look of envy.

Late in the afternoon, Rufus wobbled out of the big wagon. The smell of whiskey was strong on him. Even though he pretended he was all right, it was plain to see he was drunk.

"Feed tur-keys shum corn f'um small wagon," he said, trying to focus his eyes on the men. He seemed to have no idea that we had already fed them a second time before he came out of the wagon. "Goin' bed now," he said and staggered back to the big wagon, slipped on the wet step and fell once before he successfully climbed up inside the canvas cover.

After watching the boss retire, Zeb shook his head and John Blood muttered, "White man," with a sneer.

Bill had been watching Rufus, too, with that vacant stare which made me wonder what he really saw and how much of what he saw he understood. Who was Bill? Did he have a last name? Where did he come from? Why was he with us?

By now I had gotten to know the names of the other men, too. What I knew about them wasn't very encouraging. One called himself Joe Doaks. Another said he was Joe Jones and a third said his name was Joe Black. These three Joes usually stayed off by themselves and avoided talking with others. They never answered questions about their past or what they planned to do. Trying to be friendly one day, I asked them a lot of questions they didn't answer, except for an occasional grunt or nervous laugh.

Later, Zeb told me not to pry into others' business. He said that a fair number of bodies living in the wilderness had left the States under "uncomfortable" circumstances. They might be running away from a family responsibility, from a sheriff, or from an enemy seeking revenge for some past misdeed.

"If someone says he's Missouri Tom or Montana Jake, that's probably all he wants you to know about him," Zeb said. "You put too many questions to 'em and they might figure you're a deputy lookin' for 'em. Believe me, it's better not to ask."

I know Zeb meant well by offering that advice. But his warning actually made me all the more curious about the three Joes. After watching them for a few days, I decided that they were running from the law, probably escapees from a prison back in the States.

On the third day, the rain continued to pour as steadily as before. Red-eyed Rufus stumbled out of his wagon long enough to mumble that we would lay over for another day. Back into the wagon he went. He hadn't eaten for two or three days. Obviously, he was too pickled to care.

After feeding the turkeys, Joe Doaks slogged through the mud and into the shelter where he suggested a poker game to pass the time. The other Joes were eager to be dealt in, but Zeb said he'd play a few hands only if everyone agreed to play a popular Crow game of chance.

Joe Jones—or whoever he was—objected at first, but the others talked him into it. For a table, we laid the endgate from the small wagon across a wooden crate. Larger pieces of firewood or rocks from the cooking fire provided dry seating for the players. Zeb and the three fugitives started playing five-card stud poker with an ante limit of five cents. John Blood and Eagle stood right behind Zeb, their arms crossed on their chests. They looked like magnificent guards, alert and ready for any misdeed at the poker table.

Bill watched from a distance for the first couple of hands and then, tapping the table with his bony finger, joined the game. The way he played poker was both amusing and sad. Normally, Bill's face was blank. But after watching the game for a while, his eyes began to sparkle as I'd never seen them before. In the game, he would bid or call for more cards by tapping the table.

At first, he won an occasional game, raking in a few pennies. But then the players noticed that when Bill had a good hand, he smiled, so they'd drop out. In fact, they began joshing him whenever he started to smile.

"Oh-oh! Bill's got a powerhouse! Time for me to fold," one of the fugitives—Joe Black—joked loudly.

In those instances, Bill won the hand, but there wasn't much money in the pot because no one had anteed up. After a couple of hours, most of the players were ready to quit, so Zeb explained the hand game, which he said the Crow played.

First, he divided the crew into two equal groups and said Eagle would be the player for one group and John Blood for the other. I was on Eagle's side. Each player had a small stone that he passed back and forth between his hands. Object of the game was for the opposing team to guess which of the player's hands held the stone. If they were wrong, they surrendered one of three little sticks and the game was over when one team had all the sticks.

When the players were placing the stone, their hands moved in a blur. At first, the team members had a hard time agreeing which hand held the marker. But as the game progressed, both sides got so they called out the hand quickly. Our team behind Eagle got two of John Blood's sticks right away, but soon lost them.

"Ain't no bettin' on this game?" Joe Doaks asked.

"Sometimes, sure," Zeb said. "I've seen men bet their arrows, horses, and even their wives in the hand game. Most cases, though, not such high stakes."

"Let's all put a quarter in the pot and the winning team divides it up," Doaks said.

This time the teams couldn't agree among themselves and they all got into a big argument over whether to bet and how much. "After much bickering and swearing, they decided on a dime apiece. I didn't want to risk ten cents, but I felt I had to play, too.

Eagle fooled the other team so well we soon had all but one of their sticks. It was then John Blood's turn. His hands flashed back and forth and he sat still with his two fists in front of him.

Our team had a hard time deciding which hand to call, but finally said left hand. We were wrong.

"*He cheated!*" Joe Doaks screamed as he jerked out his pistol and put the end of the barrel against John Blood's forehead. Instantly, we were all frozen helpless.

"Put the gun away," Zeb said calmly.

"He cheated," Joe Doaks said again, this time with much less conviction. Now he realized that Eagle had a knife at his throat and Zeb had a big one ready to plunge into Doaks' belly.

"You pull that trigger and before you can blink, you'll be a pile of pemmican ready to hang out to dry," Zeb said.

Without a word, Doaks lowered his pistol, put it back in his holster and glowered at Zeb.

"This game's over," Zeb said quietly. "Everybody, pick up your money and back out of here. I'm sorry it came to this."

In silence, each man took his ten cents and left the shelter. The whole incident took place so quickly that it was hard to believe it had really happened.

Zeb put the stones and sticks back into a small buckskin bag with blue, white and yellow beadwork on the front. "Tell the boss me and the boys will be back in the morning. We need a little space after that set-to," Zeb told me.

Compared with the grim routine of playing poker, the hand game was fun until Joe Doaks blew up. I always meant to tell Zeb how much I liked it, but forgot to whenever he was around.

Toward evening, a bull train crept across the rolling prairie from the east and made camp a couple of hundred yards away from us. In all, there were thirty-two wagons pulled by teams of huge bulls. They all followed in the same deep, muddy tracks cut in the prairie grass. In charge was the same Mr. Volin I talked to in the wagon yard in Pierre the day I met Rufus. They had left Fort Pierre a week after we had and now they would pass us in the morning. How I wished I were traveling with them!

"Where's Mr. Peach?" the wagon train captain wanted to know.

"Probably asleep in his wagon," I said. "I'll get him."

"No rush. He and I have some old business to settle. We can talk in the morning. How is your drive going?"

"Just fine." I wanted to tell him how terribly boring it was to walk with a flock of brainless birds that wanted to do *anything* but follow the trail. The weather, of course, had been horrible, but Mr. Volin knew that. There was no point complaining.

"That's good. But I want you to know we could still use a cook's helper on our train. Pay is fifty cents a day and we'll be in Deadwood in eight days. Be glad to have you join us."

I wished he hadn't said that. The truth was I had often

thought about trying to walk back to Fort Pierre where I might join a wagon train like Mr. Volin's—we usually saw one every day or two—to escape Rufus's abusive mouth, the boredom of traveling so slowly, and the danger of being in a small party on the trail.

But I had agreed to stay with the herd, or flock, until it was delivered. Father would have said going back on my word was unthinkable. Sometimes Rufus wasn't so bad. After all, he was paying me a dollar a day, top wages for a man.

Seeing that I wasn't going to answer right then, Mr. Volin told me to think about it and turned to leave. He greeted Bill and then rode his horse back to his own camp.

When I went to bed that night, I found everything I owned was wet. The letter from Lucinda had been soaked so badly that it was impossible to read. Sadly, I wadded it up and threw it away. The other letter for Lucinda, given to me by the postmaster in Kankakee, was still sealed in spite of all the rainwater. I put it in a safe place to dry just before I went to sleep in my damp blanket.

During the night, the rain finally stopped. Like well-behaved children, the turkeys had all gone to bed on their own by getting up into their roosts in the trees. But with bright sunlight the next morning, they seemed eager to come down for breakfast.

We had all eaten and were getting the flock ready to move when Mr. Volin came back and talked with Rufus. Most of the time they spoke in low voices off at a distance so you couldn't hear them. From what I could gather, Rufus had once worked for Mr. Volin and owed him a large sum of money. I know Rufus was saying "Yessir" often, shaking his head in agreement and acting embarrassed a lot.

Finished with Rufus, the captain mounted his horse, came up to me and told me the offer was still open.

"Thank you, sir," I said. "Maybe some other time."

He tipped his hat and rode off.

For a moment, I stood staring after him, feeling like I had passed up my last chance ever to get away from this turkey drive. And maybe of seeing Lucinda again. As slowly as we were traveling, I worried that she would leave Deadwood before I even got there.

Chapter 7
PAYING THE TOLL

The next week was pretty ordinary on the trail. The weather was warm and clear during the day, chilly and starry at night. We settled into a routine of moving the flock of turkeys five or six miles a day, starting at sunrise, pausing to feed in the morning and again in the afternoon when we stopped a couple of hours before sunset to set up camp for the night. Sometimes Rufus led us along the main wagon and stagecoach road. That's when we saw other travelers almost every day, some headed west as we were; some returning from the Black Hills.

One night we camped near a stage stop called Cherry Creek Station, where several trails crossed because the springs there poured out ample water. Some of the crew—Rufus and the Joes—used the stop as an excuse to have a meal cooked by someone else. No one said anything, but I think we were glad they gave us a breathing spell after the ruckus over the disputed bet.

In the morning, about an hour after we had broken camp, a long procession of Sioux Indians came from the north and crossed the wagon trail in front of us. Young men rode handsome ponies and drove a herd of perhaps a hundred horses. Women, children and old men walked beside horses pulling travois heaped with bundles wrapped in buckskin and other hides. Dozens of dogs played at their heels as they marched along.

When they saw that we were trailing turkeys, some of them let out a whoop and pointed at us and started laughing wildly. Children ran up for a closer look and then dashed away. The women were the most amused by our herd of turkeys. They stared and laughed and joked with each other about what they saw. Some chortled and giggled so hard they could barely stand up as they walked by. They were so tickled that I had to laugh, too.

I noticed John Blood and Eagle Screams eyed the passing band with interest, but were careful not to greet them in any way. Zebulon Smith raised his hand and waved a sign of peace and a couple of the older Sioux men waved back, but kept on riding. Rufus stopped the wagons and we all waited while the stragglers crossed the wagon road in front of us.

For the next few days we plodded along over gently rolling hills and long, wide swales. No matter where we were, we constantly went up or down. When we reached the top of a rise, we could usually see for miles ahead, following the wagon tracks that stood out like dark strings draped over the gigantic waves of land.

The Three Fugitives and the wagon boss complained constantly about the monotony of crossing such a flat, barren territory. All that grousing amused Zeb, John Blood, and Eagle because they believed the land was always presenting something new, something fascinating, an endless gift from Mother Earth.

For me, the land was so different from Illinois. At first the treeless solitude swallowed me up and frightened me. But as I walked mile after mile through the knee-high grass, I found that I had been far lonelier on Uncle Asa's farm with neighbors on every side than I was out here. Now I was beginning to see why Zeb and his Crow companions found the land so enchanting.

As we crept westward, Rufus kept the wagons in the lead. That worked well because even though the turkeys were short on intelligence, they were smart enough to know that whenever they were given grain to eat, it came from one of the wagons.

We were near the crest of a low rise when suddenly an Indian war party rode up at a gallop and stopped in the road two hundred yards in front of us. There must have been twenty of them, lined up side by side, facing us.

Rufus let out a bellow and halted the wagons. Cussing as always, he yelled for Zeb. I was at the back of the herd, and couldn't understand the words, but it was clear that Rufus was sending Zeb out to parley with the men blocking our path.

John Blood had been riding his pony at the right flank of the herd and trotted over to where I was watching to see what would happen next.

"Cheyenne warriors," he said, nodding toward the group.

"Are they dangerous?" The instant I asked that question

I realized how dumb it sounded.

John Blood nodded. He was completely serious.

Zeb rode slowly toward the line of braves, holding up his right hand in a sign of peace. Two of the Cheyenne rode forward a short distance to meet him.

They talked for a long time. Being so far away and not knowing anything about their talking made me very uneasy. I worried that all those warriors might attack Zeb and then rush us. Finally, Zeb reined his pony about and trotted it back to the wagon.

The next thing I heard was Rufus swearing. The words weren't clear, but there was no doubt that he didn't like what Zeb was telling him about the Cheyenne.

Now Joe Doaks came by, passing the word that the boss wanted the birds moved close to the wagons and to have our weapons ready.

Zeb turned his pony and trotted back to the two forward warriors. This time their conversation lasted only a few seconds.

Again, upon hearing Zeb's report, Rufus cut loose with his choicest words to punctuate his reaction to the demands the Cheyenne were making. Clearly, Rufus wanted no part of their plan.

Three more times Zeb rode out to talk to the Cheyenne leaders, and returned to hear Rufus's abusive reply. Later, I found out that the Cheyenne first boasted they were going to kill us and take the turkeys. But Zeb convinced them that many of the Cheyenne party would die if they tried that. Then they demanded half the flock to let us go to the Black Hills. Naturally, Rufus spat on that offer.

When Zeb came back the last time, five warriors

accompanied him and rode directly to the flock. Each of them leapt off his pony, killed two turkeys and quickly remounted and left with the bleeding birds draped in front of them.

Rufus was crazy with anger. He jumped down from the main wagon, charged toward Zeb's horse and yanked the old man down in an instant. Flailing with his hamlike arms, he pummeled the old mountain man's chest and face. Just a few blows left Zeb on his back on the ground, his mouth gaping open. I knew he was dead.

So did John Blood and Eagle Screams. With knives drawn, they flew off their horses and ran at Rufus from opposite sides. With amazing deftness, the wagon boss kicked the legs of Eagle out from under him, rolling him in the grass. In the next instant, Rufus blocked John Blood's attempt to stab him in the belly, ripped the knife out of his hand and sent him sprawling in the grass. By that time Eagle was up again, ready to lunge at the wagon master.

But Eagle stopped. Rufus had yanked a pistol out of his waistband, leveled it, and was ready to shoot. Boldly, Eagle tossed his knife to the side, turned his back on Rufus, and went to Zeb's body. John Blood walked up to Eagle, said something in a low voice and they both dropped to their knees beside Zeb.

I was stunned by what had happened. Seeing Rufus kill my friend right in front of everyone shocked me. All the other crew members were numb with disbelief, too.

"What are you boneheaded yehus looking at?" Rufus yelled. "You think that old goat is dead, don't you? Shows how dumb you are." Then he turned to John Blood. "Get his mangy carcass out of here. A drink of water will fix him up. Whiskey would even be better."

Miraculously, it seemed, Zebulon Smith sat up from death and wiped a spot of blood out of the corner of his mouth. In a moment, John Blood and Eagle had him on his feet, walking unsteadily. Soon, they boosted him onto his pony and rode away a few yards to talk.

For the first time, I really hated Rufus Peach. Zebulon Smith had obviously saved our lives, getting the Cheyenne to settle for ten dopey turkeys. So how did Rufus thank him? By practically killing him. By the time we stopped to make camp, I had decided to leave this drive at the first chance that appeared.

As soon as I had coffee ready, Rufus came by for a cup. "You stick out that lower lip much farther and you're gonna step on it," he said sarcastically. "You think I did wrong, don't you?"

I simply nodded "yes."

"Well, sonny, I told that old man to do his best. I didn't tell him to give away any turkeys. What he did made me mighty mad."

"You didn't have to beat him up," I said very quietly.

"Mebbe not, but I'll guarantee he won't do that again."

Supper was awfully quiet that night. Bill loaded his plate and sat by himself on the other side of the little wagon. The Three Fugitives took theirs and hunkered down by themselves on the far side of the turkey pen. Rufus ate alone in the big wagon.

Zeb, John Blood, and Eagle ate with me, but never said a word throughout the meal. By the time we finished eating, the water was ready for doing the dishes. Zeb got out the dish towels.

"This be the last time we give you a hand in this camp," Zeb told me quietly.

"*How's that?*" What he said scared me. *How can this camp survive without Zeb and his companions?*

"We're movin' on. These young braves have seen enough civilization. What's sad is that soon it'll all be civilized. The shinin' times are gone."

"Where will you go?"

"Home." Zeb gazed at the sunset for a long time. "They're waitin' for us in the mountains. It'll be heavy winter when we get there. John Blood and Eagle want you to come with us. You can ride our pack horse until we get you one of your own."

I explained that right now I had to find my sister. After that, perhaps I could go on another adventure. His invitation was so tempting! How many boys my age were ever invited to ride with a vintage white trapper who had been adopted by the Crow? The thrill of seeing new places and meeting all kinds of new people was almost more than I could think of at the moment.

"We'll take you to Deadwood. Three, four days from now, you'll see your sister," Zeb said as a matter of fact.

That was too much to believe. Rufus had been saying it would take us at least three more weeks to get there driving turkeys.

"You sleep on it," Zeb said. "We leave at dawn. We'll see you then." He shook my hand. "Joshua, you're a fine young man. We'll be proud to have you ride with us."

Just then I had a rush of affection for the old man. I wanted to wrap my arms about him and hug him. And to tell him how badly I thought Rufus had wronged him. But, afraid of embarrassing myself, I said nothing.

The three slid up onto their ponies and rode out of our camp.

Long into the night, there was no sleep for me. Part of the time, my head was spinning with joy over seeing my sister in a few days instead of weeks. There were so many things I had to tell her. I could hardly wait.

Also, my head was bursting with dreams of traveling with Zebulon Smith, John Blood, and Eagle Screams, not only to Deadwood and the Black Hills, but on west into Montana Territory and the home of the Mountain Crow. What could be more exciting? Dangerous? Maybe, but with an old mountain man like Zeb, I'd soon learn the tricks of surviving, of getting along with the people.

Then I looked at these wonderful dreams through my father's eyes. His greatest lesson was always treating the other fellow right. Now he spoke to me though my conscience.

Rufus Peach is a rough man, impatient, sometimes unfair. He never said this trip would be a picnic. In fact, he insisted no one could quit once the drive started. Now three of them are pulling out. In truth, they are being driven out by Rufus's foul disposition and the hostility of the other crew members.

If Zeb, John Blood and Eagle Screams leave, only Rufus, Bill, the Three Fugitives and I will be left. If I leave, the crew will be without a cook and only four herders. They won't be able to manage.

But it's all Rufus's fault.

He gave me a job when no one else would. He has a

wicked mouth and a vile spirit, but does he deserve to lose nearly half of his crew overnight? Why are you even worrying about that heartless drunk? He'd leave you in the blink of an eye if it suited his purposes.

But I'm not him. I'm Joshua Greene. My word is good.

So for most of the night, I tossed and turned, wrestling with this stew of thoughts. Sometimes my spirit soared with Zeb, John Blood and Eagle Screams in marvelous dreams. And at times my heart welled up so I fairly cried with joy to see my sister again.

But a deal is a deal. I took this job, agreeing to see the drive through. Doing the right thing isn't always exciting. But it is right. With that thought, I finally went to sleep.

Zeb woke me by gently tugging at my shoulder in the eerie light of early dawn.

"We best be pullin' out now," he said quietly.

"I want to go with you, but I promised to stay," I said.

Zeb nodded. "I understand. Well, best of luck to you." In an instant, he was gone.

A minute or so later, I heard his pony trot off into the distance. Swallowing hard, I hoped I hadn't made another big mistake sticking with the drive.

Chapter 8
No help

Rufus had a foul-mouthed tantrum when he found out that Zeb, John Blood, and Eagle Screams had left the drive. In his rage, he called them all kinds of obscene names, some of which I had never heard before. He seemed to be carrying on to warn anyone else who wanted to leave that they would pay a high price for it.

"Why did they leave?" he asked me five different times.

At first I hesitated to answer, fearing that he'd lambaste me, too. But Rufus insisted on knowing, so I told him, "You beat him up. He saved most of the flock. And our skins, too."

"What do you know, you boneheaded greenhorn?"

Well, you asked me, I said under my breath, packing up the cooking gear. *Who'll help me now?* Zeb had faithfully appeared after meals to finish the dishes and pack up the supplies in the morning. Although John Blood and Eagle had worked in silence, they were able assistants.

All the while that Zeb and the Crows were a part of the crew, Rufus had shown a pointed dislike for them. Now Rufus continued to curse the three for every weakness he could imagine. It struck me that he couldn't stand them because they were not like him. He twisted these differences into saying they weren't even human.

When Rufus told us to move out, I thought he'd give us some orders for handling the flock with a smaller crew. But, no, he didn't see any need to talk about being short-handed. As always, he climbed up on the wagon and cracked his whip to get us going.

Bill and Joe Doaks rode at the left side of the flock while the other Joes—Jones and Black—directed their horses along the right flank. I followed up the rear, still the only drover on foot. This time the birds seemed to be on their best behavior.

When we stopped at mid-morning to graze both the bulls and the turkeys, Rufus bawled out the Three Fugitives for riding too close to the turkeys, trying to cripple the poor birds. They returned the attack with a silent, icy stare and mouths that sagged at the corners with cold contempt. I figured they had probably taken many insults from hostile jailers, so they knew how to keep quiet.

Then Rufus turned his wicked tongue on me. "You think you'll find your runaway sister in Deadwood, huh?"

"I hope so."

"I wouldn't be hopin' that. I'd sure hate to find *my* sister there," he declared.

"*What do you mean?*" I didn't like the way he was talking.

"I mean that any woman that goes to the gold camps ain't one to brag about. They hang out in the saloons and make their livin'—"

"My sister isn't like that," I protested.

"Then why'd she go to Deadwood? Why'd she run away from a perfectly good job in Illi-noise? You ought to be ashamed." He spat a thin stream of tobacco juice and walked away.

The big lout. He doesn't know anything about my sister, Lucinda. Now I really wish I had gone with the Volin wagon train a few days ago or with Zeb and the Crows this morning. Rufus is mad at them, but he is taking out his anger on us who stayed.

That afternoon, Rufus made fun of the Three Fugitive's horse, donkey, and mule. True, their mounts were of terribly low quality and in poor condition. If they had actually bought those nags, they had paid too much at any price.

The three Joes sulked, but did not reply to the boss's badgering.

"I been thinkin' about your sister," he said, turning to me. "When we get to Deadwood, I'm gonna look her up."

"I'll thank you to stop insulting my sister," I said tightly.

"O-o-o-h? Does our little cook have a touchy spot?" he asked, roaring with laughter and adding his favorite cuss words.

"You don't know her. So quit saying things about her."

Again, he howled with laughter. But no one else was laughing. The Three Fugitives were all stirred up by his slurs about their mounts. They conveniently frowned in directions away from Rufus. Bill, the mute soldier, seemed to pick up on the tense situation. He was more jittery than usual, fidgeting with the buttons on his old blue coat. His eyes blinked nervously, but as always, he looked off into nowhere and listened to no one. At least not in our camp.

"What's her name?" Rufus wanted to know.

"What's your *mother's* name?" I asked in a surly tone.

After muttering a few words I'd never repeat, he let the matter drop. He filled his tin cup with coffee and swaggered back to the big wagon, where he probably added a slosh of liquor.

After supper I asked Bill to help me clean up the dishes. I got out a towel and handed it to him, but he just stood there, acting like he didn't know what to do with it. When I was almost done, I took the towel out of his hand.

Suddenly I felt lonely and sad. Zeb had been the only man on the drive that had offered any friendship and now he was gone. Eagle Screams might have become a friend, too, if we could have talked to each other. Now I remembered Zeb once said, "Out here, you need a partner to watch your back and help you in the deep water."

During the past year, whenever someone had mistreated me, someone else befriended me. Uncle Asa tried to make me his slave. But the postmaster in Kankakee saw to it I got my mail, which got me out of there. Ole the Swede showed me generosity on the riverboat *Far West* just when I was beginning to think there were no good people left on earth. And Zebulon Smith helped at mealtime when no one else would.

With Rufus turning uglier, who could I turn to for friendship? Bill? Poor Bill was out of touch with the whole world, probably even himself. One of the Three Fugitives? Not likely. They had their squabbles, but they were partners and took care of each other.

For the next three days, Rufus was more and more on the prod. He found fault with everything anyone did—it was either too fast or two slow. Or simply done wrong. When I served boiled potatoes at supper, Rufus said they should have been fried. If I made biscuits, he wanted corn bread. He was acting like a spoiled child.

Only Bill escaped the boss's constant bullying. Apparently Rufus knew it would do no good to hound the old soldier who practically never reacted to anything.

One morning while we stopped to let the bulls and turkeys graze, Joe Doaks stretched out in the shade of the wagon to take a short nap. This mid-morning break had been a quiet time every day we were on the road and we drovers were free to do anything we wanted if the birds didn't drift away. Then, we had to keep them from scattering.

Doaks had just drifted off to sleep when Rufus walked up and kicked him in the ribs. Doaks sat up with a jolt and growled, "What'd you do that fur?"

"You lazy good-fur-nothin', I'm not paying you to sleep. "Get out there and watch them turkeys."

"Go watch 'em yourself!"

"What'd you say?"

"You heard me. Go watch your stupid turkeys yourself."

Rufus was getting mighty red in the face by now. Even the back of his neck looked hot and angry. He leaned over and took a swipe at Joe Doak's face, but Doaks ducked and rolled away from Rufus. Then he scrambled to his feet and backed away cautiously.

Rufus advanced; Doaks retreated.

For a moment I thought Rufus would go after Doaks like he had Zebulon Smith. Doaks said he didn't want any trouble; he was going to watch the herd. Even so, Rufus ranted at him with foul words.

That night, after supper, the Three Fugitives walked a ways from camp and got into a big argument that ended in a gunshot. Rufus ran up and waded into them as if they were unruly children.

Later I found out that Rufus bawled them out for firing a gun. He said the sound of a gunshot traveled a long way on the prairie and there was no telling who might come to investigate. Like Sioux or Cheyenne warriors. Then he tried to take their pistols away from them, but the three refused. When Rufus insisted, they all three pulled their guns on the boss and said they wouldn't travel through this hostile country without their weapons.

For once, Rufus backed down. But not without a full measure of grumbling and cussing.

As I was cleaning up after supper, Bill showed up and extended one arm. I found a dish towel and draped it over the limb. He glanced at it for a moment and went on staring into the gathering darkness. He just stood there in silence. It was eerie. It gave me the willies. I wished he'd leave, but he didn't. The moment I finished and took the towel from his arm, he vanished into the night.

Bill's melancholy, the absence of Zeb, John Blood, and Eagle, and Rufus's nagging everyone were dragging my spirits down. The ugliness of life in our camp made me daydream about life back home with Mother, Father, and Lucinda, and its warm comfort. But the truth was those days were gone forever. Realizing it dashed the memory and brought back the ache in my heart and the lump in my throat. The fact was that I'd never see Mother and Father again on this earth. I just couldn't think of that.

Sometimes as I walked along with the wind in my face, the fresh touch would remind me of the way Mother used to brush my hair out of my eyes with her hand. I wondered if she knew where I was. One night I lay on my blanket and gazed up at the countless stars overhead. *Which of those stars are Mother and Father? Do they see me? Do they see Lucinda at this moment, too?* My eyes filled with tears. I wiped them away with my fists, turned over and went to sleep, exhausted from another day of walking across Dakota Territory.

The next day, I was trailing the back of the flock as always, plodding along and feeling lost when Joe Doaks rode up.

"Mail this for me, kid." He handed me a letter, complete with a stamp on it.

I didn't know what to say. He'd have a chance to mail it just as soon as I would. "Sure, I'll be glad to mail it. But why don't you wait and do it yourself?"

"Can't say right now. Just do it, all right?" He was getting a little short with me.

"Yessir." I pushed the letter into my pocket and kept walking.

When we halted for our afternoon stop for grazing, the Three Fugitives rode together over a small rise. I guessed they were riding down to a small creek just out of sight. Wherever they went, they never came back. At first I wasn't alarmed. They had always stayed apart from the rest of the crew. And with Rufus being on the peck, their avoiding the boss seemed normal, too. So, I gave their absence little thought until they had been gone for nearly an hour. Then I told Rufus I thought they had pulled out.

"They ain't got enough guts to do that," Rufus scoffed.

"What if they don't come back?"

"They will. They're scared to death of this country. By dark, those spineless slugs will be right beside us."

I wanted to argue with Rufus that this time it was different. That someone should go after them. They were half of our crew. Without them, we'd be unable to travel.

Seeing that the three Joes were not back when it was time to start the afternoon trek, Rufus decided we had better put up the wire pen for the turkeys and camp where we were. With Bill's help, we set it up and herded the turkeys inside.

What are we going to do? I was almost in a panic. Rufus was unusually quiet. I think he must have realized what a serious mess we were in. This time, he didn't ask why the three Joes had left. He must have known that they had reached their limit on putting up with his mistreatment. Our crew of nine was now down to Rufus, Bill and myself. Considering Bill's mental state, that added up to a man, an invalid and a boy. Hardly the kind of company needed to drive eight hundred turkeys across this dangerous land.

By the next morning, we knew for certain that the Three Fugitives were not coming back. Still, Rufus insisted on going on. After breakfast, we took down the wire pen and loaded it before he started the bull team and wagons at the lead. Bill and I trailed along at the sides near the back of the herd. Again, the birds cooperated. For the first hour.

Then we crossed a series of hills and went along a valley where there were millions of grasshoppers that had somehow survived the frosty nights. The turkeys went crazy chasing and pecking off grasshoppers. They ran every direction, scattering like quail. I dashed all over the place trying to keep them together. Almost as suddenly as they appeared, the insects were gone, either eaten by the pebbly-faced birds or they had escaped.

By nightfall we had the birds back in the pen. I was exhausted from running all day, chasing loose turkeys. We had traveled less than three miles for all that work.

"We can't go on this way," I told Rufus at supper. "We have to have more help. Someone has to go back to Fort Pierre or ahead to the Black Hills to hire more drovers."

"Can't." Rufus wouldn't say why not.

"Then hire some of the travelers on the trail."

"You can't trust any of the scum on the road," Rufus said, swearing. "'Sides, we ain't got time fur runnin' around, lookin' fur help. We waste many days and we miss the Thanksgiving market for these birds."

Oh, fine, I told myself. *At the rate we're going, we might be there in time for next year's Thanksgiving market.*

The Three Fugitives had taken care of night guard after Zeb and the young Crows left. Now it was up to Rufus,

Bill, and me to protect the birds from any nighttime prowlers. Rufus told me to take a pistol he had in the big wagon. I refused. The gun was big and heavy. Although I wasn't afraid of it, I felt that shooting at some noise in the dark would be foolish. Besides, having a loaded firearm in your hands could cause an accident.

Before turning in for the night, I circled the turkey pen, pushing my hands deep into my jacket pockets. There I found the letter Joe Doaks had asked me to mail. Because I had forgotten about it, I hadn't mentioned it to Rufus. Now if I told him about it, he'd probably tear it up out of anger. *I'll just mail it when I can or give it to a traveler headed east,* I decided.

The next morning, Rufus said we'd lay over for a day where we were. He instructed us to leave the turkeys in their pen all day, but to feed them grain from the big wagon and make sure they had plenty of water. Without saying anything more to Bill and me, he went to saddle Bill's gray mule, but the animal reared and snapped her teeth and kicked until Rufus gave up. Then Bill saddled the animal and held her head tight while the boss climbed on. The mule started with several bucks and snorts. Hanging on tight, Rufus rode her out of camp.

Now the crew was down to Bill and myself. If robbers or a war party came along, they'd have an easy time of taking the herd, the wagons, and everything else. I wished Rufus would have at least told us when he'd be back.

Mostly to keep my mind off being alone out on the prairie, I hauled buckets of grain for the birds and watered them. Everywhere I went, Bill was right beside me or behind me. He, too, seemed to be uneasy about our situation. When I finished the work, I sat down on the tongue of the big wagon to rest. Bill sat right beside me.

"Bill, I'm feeling awful edgy this morning. How are you doing?"

Nothing.

"Bill, did you ever dream you'd be crossing the wilds of Dakota with eight hundred turkeys?"

He stared off at the distant horizon, silent as ever.

"Bill, I hear they've just crowned you King of France. I'm sure you'll be one of the greatest monarchs ever in Europe," I said sarcastically. Almost instantly, I regretted saying it.

He didn't mind; in fact, he probably never heard me.

Toward noon, I could see someone coming from the west. At first it looked like a tiny black ant creeping toward us. In time, I could see it was a wagon and three mounted riders. I prayed they weren't bringing trouble.

Chapter 9
NIGHT VISITORS

The coming travelers turned out to be Rufus and three men from the next stage station up the road. The father wore an immense red handlebar mustache and his two burly sons talked all the time. At first I was pleased to have their company, but it didn't take long for them to wear out the welcome I had felt for them.

Rufus never bothered to introduce the new help. When I told them who I was, they didn't care. In fact, the brothers went on talking to each other as if I weren't there. The boss said these men would be with us for only a few days. After that, we'd hire new crew members as best we could.

Their name was Johnson and they turned out to be champion bellyachers. Even though they were large, strong men, they complained about the hard work of putting up and taking down the wire pen for the birds, the boredom of moving at a snail's pace, the rough road, and how nerve-wracking the endless wind was.

To their credit, they left Bill alone.

But they insulted my cooking endlessly. The coffee was too weak. The beans were overcooked. The biscuits were too brown. The stew didn't have enough meat in it. Of course, that didn't keep them from hogging down three-fourths of the vittles I cooked.

The new men took over night watch. I suspected they all went to sleep early because I never heard any movement after they started. In fact, their first night on guard proved to me how poorly they were guarding us.

By now, our food supplies had dwindled, leaving room in the small wagon, so I started sleeping there. It was out of the wind and if it rained or snowed, my bedding would stay nice and dry.

Worn out from a day on the trail, starting with cooking breakfast and ending with supper, I crawled into my bed early. When I climbed up into the wagon, I noticed the moon was still nearly full, but would set in the west in a couple of hours. There was some comfort in being able to see objects in the moonlight. Almost as soon as I pulled my blanket up over my head, I fell asleep.

Something tugged at my foot. More asleep than awake, I pushed it away with my other foot and drifted off again. Next, something pushed against my shoulder. Remembering where I was, I sat up bolt straight, terrified.

Someone was in the wagon with me! I wanted to scream for help, but nothing came out of my mouth. When I tried to get to my feet, the person held me down.

"Shh. It's me."

"Who?" I must have sounded like a frightened owl.

"John Blood."

"What are you doing here?"

"We have come to talk. We must go."

"Go? Where?"

"You come." He took hold of my wrist and pulled gently toward the opening in the wagon cover.

At first, I resisted. Going out into the night with John Blood seemed unwise. But then I told myself I'd get to see Zebulon Smith again. So I pulled on my shoes and laced them up, grabbed my jacket and slid out of the wagon.

John Blood didn't waste a second getting out of camp. I followed him closely up a gentle slope and then over the top, out of sight from the turkey pen and the wagons.

Eagle Screams was waiting, holding the horses.

"Where's Zeb?" I asked, feeling alarmed. It had been five days since he and the young Crow men had left the drive, but I expected him to be here, too.

"He who is not here has gone to a new place."

"*What*?" I didn't like getting a riddle for an answer.

"Gray Beard died."

I had never heard John Blood call Zeb by any name in English, but there was little doubt now that he was speaking about his grandfather.

"How did he die?" I asked desperately.

"He was an old man."

I asked if Zeb had died because of Rufus's attack. At first John Blood didn't understand what I was asking. After three tries, he murmured that no one had killed Gray Beard.

Disappointment and sadness flooded me and I had to

gulp air to stay afloat. I wanted to know where he was buried, but didn't know how to ask. Finally, I said, "I am sad he is gone."

The two Crow stood in silence for a respectful moment.

"We have watched your camp. More men have quit. We are staying near to watch and come running to fight."

"You would help us if we needed help?"

John Blood smiled. "We are friends. You *will* need help."

When I asked him what he was talking about, John tried to explain, but I didn't understand. Eagle Screams said something to him in Crow and John Blood tried again. Now I understood that our trail drive was moving into some kind of trap.

"There's a Cheyenne camp," he said, pointing west, up the road.

"But Rufus and the Johnsons just came from the west. They would have seen such a camp," I argued.

"These Cheyenne just came as the sun was going away."

Now I was getting suspicious. *What do they want from me? Why have they lured me out of camp, anyway? Have they been watching our progress, looking for a time to attack? Would they really lend us a hand if we needed it?* The fact that Zeb wasn't here made me edgy, too. He had always been a link between me and them and that made it possible for us to understand each other. Eagle was holding the reins to Zeb's horse, which I recognized in the moonlight.

"I'd better go back to camp," I said a little too hastily. I hoped they hadn't noticed my rising fear.

"We show you. Come." John Blood swung up onto his pony in a fluid movement. Eagle handed me the rein to

Zeb's horse and slid up onto his own. Both waited patiently for me to mount. While they rode bareback, Zeb had always used an Indian saddle that had short stirrups. Awkwardly, I climbed up. *If John Blood and Eagle try anything funny, at least I might escape on this horse.*

For a distance we walked the horses slowly until we were out of earshot of our camp. Beyond another rise, we set out at a gallop and rode hard for two or three miles. Then we slowed to a walk again. By now the moon had sunk so it was just above the horizon. We stopped in a draw, dismounted and left the ponies with Eagle.

John Blood said softly, "Come."

With almost perfect silence, he walked through the grass so fast I had a hard time keeping up. To my embarrassment, I tripped and fell once. After that, John Blood went more slowly. As we came to the crest of a hill, we went down onto our hands and knees and crept forward into a clump of tall grass. Here, we had a view of the valley below. Without speaking, he pointed to it.

Barely, I could make out several horses in a tight group.

An instant later, John Blood put his hand on my shoulder and pushed me down, flat onto the ground, into the coarse grass. Two men walked by so close to our heads that we could have reached out and touched their feet. I could sense the tension John Blood was feeling, with knife drawn, ready to spring into deadly combat in a split second. In that instant, I thought I was going to cough or sneeze, but somehow I held my breath so tightly that absolutely no air came out. As quickly as they appeared, the Cheyenne sentries were gone. We had escaped them by only inches.

John Blood waited for a moment and then we backtracked to where Eagle was waiting with the horses.

"That was a close call!" I whispered excitedly.

John Blood nodded. "Those are Cheyenne warriors. They're coming to take more big birds. And maybe kill the bird walkers."

Obviously, we would walk right into their ambush if we stayed on the main wagon road with our trail drive. But then, how did John Blood know what the Cheyenne had in mind? Had he talked to them? Zeb had told me that the Crow were unpopular with the Cheyenne and the Sioux because some Crow braves had served as scouts for the U.S. Cavalry. I had to trust that John Blood was telling the truth.

"Why did you come back? Why are you helping us?"

John Blood laughed softly. "You are a friend. Gray Beard told me to watch out for Josh-you-ah."

"And what do *you* say?"

"I say you are brave. You work for that hard man, Rufus, without complaining. You keep your word. You don't run from the Cheyenne guards that almost step on us. That's plenty courage."

That made me feel good. Until now, I had believed that John Blood saw me as a weakling.

"Do you miss Gray Beard?"

John Blood pressed his fist against his chest and said, "A great sadness hurts here when I think that he is gone."

"Me, too. He was a fine man. I'm proud that he was my friend."

John Blood took a long time to digest what I had said. In the darkness it was impossible to tell what he was thinking. But I know that during that moment we mourned our loss together.

"You come with us now?" he asked.

"Where?"

"Black Hills. Big Horn Mountains. Beautiful land, beautiful people."

"I wish I could. I have to stay with Rufus Peach, Bill, and those dumb turkeys. I must finish the drive."

John Blood accepted what I said. He hopped up onto his pony and waited for Eagle and me to mount, too. Quietly, we walked the horses a long distance and then galloped along the wagon road again, careening through the darkness with exhilarating swiftness. Somehow they knew when to slow the ponies and go on foot.

Eagle and I said goodbye again. We shook hands and John Blood led me back up the slope that overlooked our camp. He stayed with me all the way back to the small wagon, making sure I didn't have any trouble with the night guards. Most likely, they were fast asleep. Or maybe we really were so quiet that they couldn't hear us.

"Thank you, John Blood. I'll tell Rufus to go another way."

"We watch," he said solemnly.

"Will I see you again?"

"Maybe so." He cuffed my shoulder lightly and vanished into the darkness without a sound.

Chapter 10
CIRCLING

Upon awakening the next morning, I went straight to Rufus Peach and told him we would be attacked if we continued driving the flock on the wagon road. In response, he gave me a pained look.

"How do you know that?"

"I saw them."

"*How?*" he asked grumpily.

From the moment I returned to camp last night, I feared that no one would believe me. If that happened, then Rufus would mindlessly march us into the Cheyenne war party with deadly results. How could I convince him? The boss was waiting for my answer. I decided it was best to tell him the incredible truth, exactly as it happened.

"Them Injuns came back? How about the old trapper?"

"After they left us, Zeb died. John Blood said he died quietly in his sleep—of old age."

Rufus thought about this for a moment and then asked suspiciously, "Why would a couple of young Injuns want to help us?"

"I asked them that. The Cheyenne are enemies of the Crow. They said they wanted to help us."

Rufus salted his thinking aloud with a heavy dose of profanity. He said he would discuss the situation with the Johnsons.

"If you don't believe me, send someone ahead to scout. We are wasting precious time. We should eat quick and leave another way."

"I didn't say I didn't believe you," he said testily. "I'm just not sure what to do about it. Go fix us some breakfast. We'll talk about it when we eat."

That didn't make me feel much better. If the Johnsons lived at a stage stop out here, they might think I was sounding a false alarm. After all, I was just a kid.

I whipped up a big batch of biscuits and gravy made with bacon. For those who wanted it on their biscuits, we also had a tin of honey. We all sat and ate together.

Rufus cleared his throat and then cussed out the turkeys for getting us into such a pickle. He admitted he had never been in such a spot as this and that we had to pull together to come out okay.

"Seems young Joshua here did some forward reconnoitering last night and found a band of Cheyenne laying across the road a few miles ahead, just waiting to pluck us and the turkeys."

This really got the Johnsons' attention. They leaned forward to hear more.

Bill had gotten honey on his fingers and was licking it

off. This crisis didn't touch him. Once in a while he looked at Rufus as he talked, maybe because it was one of those rare times that Rufus was worried.

"They probably plan to come at us from behind the Grindstone Buttes," the elder Johnson said. "It's a poor place for an ambush, but it's better than out on the flats. Might be wise to circle north for two, three days and pick up the road again farther west." As seriously as he was taking this situation, I guessed problems in the past made him cautious.

"Jist what did you see?" he asked me.

"In the moonlight, it looked like about thirty horses, held in a tight bunch. John Blood said there were between twenty and thirty Cheyenne warriors. I didn't see them myself."

"Did they have a fire?"

"No."

"Did they have a night guard out?"

"Yes." But I figured he didn't need to know how close the Cheyenne sentries came to catching us.

"Well, Mr. Peach, these might be the same fellows who got a taste of your turkeys before and decided they want some more," the elder Mr. Johnson said. "Unless you can shake 'em off your trail, you just may have to fight 'em off."

Rufus ordered Mr. Johnson to drive his wagon next to the big wagon leading the drive. They'd both have rifles and if anyone got in their way, they would greet them with a hail of bullets.

We started out before sunrise. For nearly a hundred miles now, we had crept across the Dakota plains, inching up gentle slopes and down the other side, always at a painful crawl. The brisk fall morning was made for moving faster, and for the first couple of miles, we walked right along. But then the sun rose higher and lulled the turkeys into a lazy stroll. It seemed like they had to cock their heads and look at every blade of grass along the way.

The other men were bristling with firearms. All three of the Johnsons were carrying rifles, as was Rufus. The boss apparently had strapped around Bill's waist a wide black belt with a holster stamped "U. S." on the flap. You couldn't tell whether there was a pistol inside, but I supposed so since the holster weighted down that side of the belt.

I wondered what Bill would do if someone started shooting at us. Again Rufus told me to take a big revolver, too. When I said "no," he muttered that I'd be mighty sorry if things got hot.

Before I had gone to live with Uncle Asa, I had enjoyed shooting a small caliber squirrel gun that Father had given me for Christmas. In the fall of the year, we'd go hunting, but seldom brought home any game for the dinner table. The pleasure of tramping through the woods, enjoying the colorful leaves, the warm sun, and laughing together was enough to make hunting fun for us. Oh, it was exciting to shoot, too. The rifles would fire with sharp little cracking noises. Sometimes we set up bottles and shot at them; other times we took potshots at dead limbs on trees to see if we could bring them down. After some practice, I could usually hit what I wanted to.

A couple of weeks after I arrived at Uncle Asa's, we butchered two hogs. My uncle used a rifle to dispatch the first animal and then handed the weapon to me and told me to shoot the other one. I said, "No thanks," but he got so ugly about it that I had to do what he said. Carefully, I took aim. But I couldn't hold the rifle steady; I was shaking terribly. Finally, I shot. Instead of ending the animal's life instantly, I had wounded him above one ear, serious enough for blood to trickle down his jowl. The hog squealed in terror and looked right at me.

I tried to hand the rifle back to Uncle Asa, but he said no, I had to finish it myself. To my horror, he was enjoying this spectacle with a twisted grin on his face. By now, I felt sick. Carefully, I drew a bead again and finished the execution. That's when I swore I'd never kill anything again. So, when the trail boss told me to carry a gun, I declined. But I never tried to explain why.

By midmorning when we stopped to graze the bulls, Rufus told us to put out some grain for the turkeys. We had come more than three miles, the best distance we'd ever made early in the day.

While we paused, the younger Johnson brother rode out in a wide circle to look for signs of the Cheyenne war party. An hour later, he returned, saying he had seen no one, friend or foe. That was small comfort. As we inched across the prairie, I thought about the Cheyenne warriors and their swift ponies. There are only six of us. Actually four, if you took out Bill and myself as probable noncombatants. Odds of four against thirty determined fighters frightened me. John Blood said he and Eagle would be watching and come to help. Even with them, Bill and me joining the ranks, that was eight against thirty, still little chance of surviving.

As we passed the time while the bulls grazed, Mr. Johnson regaled us with stories of the many scrapes with Indians he had survived. He had been a bullwhacker all over the plains. For a time he drove bulls up the Bozeman Trail in Montana Territory until that route was closed. He had been a teamster for the army in Kansas and had even been with Custer's Expedition to the Black Hills in 1874, the year gold was discovered there.

Because of his advanced age and many years on the frontier, Mr. Johnson reminded me of Zeb. But the old trapper always marveled at the wonders he had seen in the mountains, on the rivers, on the plains. He had only good words for the scores of people he had met, no matter whether they were red, white, black, or yellow.

In contrast, Mr. Johnson bragged about how much smarter than anyone else he and his fellow freighters had been. He talked about the land, the great herds of buffalo, and other animals as things that had to be conquered or killed to be worth counting. And if he and his friends—especially the U. S. Cavalry—hadn't fought for the land, it would have gone to waste. They were paving the way, he said, for civilization.

Zeb's version was that the land and the native people there were perfect and had been so for centuries. They had welcomed the first white men because there was plenty for everyone. But the trickle of "civilized" people, mostly from Europe, had turned into an invading flood. I guess it was a good thing that Zeb and the Crow youths had left the drive. Had they been here with Mr. Johnson, there probably would have been trouble between them.

Mr. Johnson liked to talk just as much as Zeb had.

One big difference was that Rufus listened to Mr. Johnson's stories and always agreed with them.

Before we started out again, Rufus came up to me and said, "Take this," thrusting a big pistol toward me.

"No, thanks. I might have an accident with it."

Cussing softly, the boss kept the revolver, climbed back up on the big wagon and led off for the afternoon leg for the day's drive. Even though he had not forced me to take the weapon, I expected he soon would. If the danger of attack did really worsen, I would want some protection of my own, anyway.

Nearly three weeks on the trail had changed me. For the first week, I was scared out of my skin of everything I saw. John Blood and Eagle Screams had terrified me. The coyotes' and wolves' howling at night jangled my nerves. Rufus's fowl language and constant badgering the crew kept me jumping all the time, too.

Right away, Zebulon Smith saw how frightened I was. Gently, he told me it was a waste of energy to jump at shadows. Most things, he said, survived by avoiding danger. And that's what we were doing right now— tiptoeing around a superior force.

In this company, I was alone in one respect. Everyone else had a horse or mule or team of oxen that transported them. I walked. I had walked all the way from the Missouri River and now I was proud of traveling all those miles afoot. In fact, I looked forward to finishing the drive walking. But under attack, I would have no horse to whisk me away in retreat if necessary. Only Rufus was as much of a sitting duck as myself. But he would have some cover in the wagon.

The Johnson brothers rode at the flanks of the flock and I trailed behind. They cradled their rifles in their laps as they walked their horses. Their eyes constantly scanned the horizon and the nearby draws for any sign of trouble.

Perhaps for added protection, Mr. Johnson now followed the flock in his wagon instead of leading the procession as he had before. It would have been nice if he had offered me half the seat beside him. For a time, he watched the prairie with the eyes of a hawk. But after an hour or so, his head fell forward, a sure sign that he had fallen asleep at the reins of his team.

Bill didn't seem to know where he fit in the drive any longer. For a while he was up front with the tandem wagons. Then he rode near the younger Johnson brother, but neither of them spoke to each other. Then he came back and rode parallel to Mr. Johnson's wagon. By now, the old gentleman with the huge reddish mustache was snoring loudly. That noise seemed to irritate Bill, so he rode farther away from the wagon. Before long, he was an outrider about two hundred yards to the side of Mr. Johnson's wagon.

Bill had moved around like that before, but had never wandered far. I figured in time he would drift back in closer to the herd. Within a half hour, he was up front with Rufus, near the big wagon. Although Bill didn't seem to be aware of most things, his mule, Jenny, was always alert and seemed to have more sense than the old soldier himself.

Except for the one time that Rufus rode her, no one touched Jenny but Bill. No one else could saddle her. One morning, one of the Three Fugitives tried to put his own saddle on the mule to see if he could get a rise out of Bill, who watched quietly.

The mule took a bite out of the seat of Joe's pants. The way the fugitive hollered, the jenny must have gotten a nice slice of rump, too.

Everyone else got a big laugh out of Joe's misfortune. Almost instantly, Bill walked over, laid on his saddle blanket and saddle and cinched up. With no problem at all, he slipped a bit into her mouth and rode off as though nothing had happened.

That day we traveled eight miles by Rufus's reckoning. Until now we had made a record of six and an average of five miles. Everyone was still edgy, of course, watching the distance as if they were expecting storm clouds or worse to approach.

While we were penning up the turkeys, the older Johnson brother rode out a mile or two and shot a deer. I thought the sound of gunshot would have given away our whereabouts, but no one else said anything, other than to express their gratitude for the fresh venison steaks.

Rufus ordered the men to take turns on night watch and to make sure there was no fire after dark. Lucky for me, he didn't put me on guard. I had to do dishes alone, but that was all right. I'd be asleep in my bedroll while the others cursed the night chill.

Just before I went to sleep, I remembered that John Blood had said they might see me again before he and Eagle left for home in Montana Territory. Were they nearby? Something in my heart told me they were looking out for us.

The last thing I thought about before drifting off was Lucinda's smile. How I hoped she was safe tonight.

Chapter 11
BUSTED

That night, John Blood and Eagle Screams came to our camp again and got me out of bed. We walked far enough away from the wagons and turkey pen so we could talk without anyone in camp hearing us. Eagle was tickled by something. By the waning moonlight, I could see his broad smile. At times he laughed softly to himself. He said something in Crow to John Blood.

"Eagle laughs because the bird walkers travel slower than the turtle, but get away from the Cheyenne," John Blood explained. Eagle had spent the day spying on the Cheyenne war party. He watched them all morning as they waited for us to arrive at Grindstone Buttes. When they realized that we were not coming into their ambush, they sent out two riders to locate us. An hour or so later, they returned with the amazing story that we had vanished.

Because we had made no effort to hide our tracks when we left the main road, it would have been easy for them to follow the clear tracks of the wagon wheels and catch up with us. But for some reason, they didn't, luckily for us.

John Blood said the Cheyenne warriors got into an argument and finally settled into a quiet meeting of the group hunkered down in a circle on the ground. That session ended with their mounting their ponies and riding off to the south, away from the wagon road.

"No longer hungry for tur-keys," John Blood said, smiling. "Gray Beard told us, 'Watch the Cheyenne and help Josh-you-ah.' Now the Cheyenne are gone, so Eagle and I can go home to our people."

That sounded like goodbye to me. Now I regretted not spending more time talking to John Blood and Eagle when I had had the chance. John Blood no longer seemed so fierce, even though I knew he was a strong fighter. Eagle had always impressed me as friendly, curious, and good-humored. But he, too, was powerfully built and well trained as a warrior. They were a few years older then me, though, and that difference might have been a barrier, anyway.

"Gray Beard sent a present for you," John Blood said, stepping back from Eagle and me and toward his pony. He came back with a large bundle. "It's a fine buffalo robe to keep you warm when winter comes." He thrust the large bundle into my arms. It was so large and heavy it almost knocked me down.

"Good-bye, Josh-you-ah," John Blood said solemnly.

Eagle said something in Crow. Instantly, I knew he

had said, "Peace," as he and John Blood slid up onto their ponies, turned, and rode off quietly into the night.

I felt like a little brother being left behind. I almost cried out, "Wait! I wanna go with you!" But something inside stopped me. I knew we had to go our separate ways, but the word "if" kept bobbing up in my mind, with new excuses to join them.

A lump in my throat hurt all the way down into my chest as I carried the huge tanned buffalo skin back to the small wagon. The robe was like a great comforter covered on one side with woolly hair instead of being stuffed with down. It was my keepsake from Zebulon Smith, trapper, explorer, mountain man, and Crow. Inside the wagon, I curled up in the soft skin and fell asleep in seconds.

The next morning, a chilly wind blew out of the northwest, making walking with the flock miserable. For a while I considered telling Rufus and Mr. Johnson what John Blood had told me about the Cheyenne, but I decided that wasn't necessary.

When you spend day after day with eight hundred turkeys, it's amazing how well you get to know them. Of all those birds, only two toms were really big, nearly three feet tall to the tops of their heads. The others were about six inches shorter, except for the few runts. Most of the hens were smaller, too.

Those two big birds showed the greatest character. Take Buzzard, for instance. He was the crankiest one of the whole flock. His entire head was bright blue and featherless. Wherever he went, others scrambled out of his way. When he ate, no other bird challenged him for a share. A couple of times he went running in the wrong direction and I had to sprint like an antelope to get around him. Once he turned on me, flapping his wings to attack. But as he got closer, he changed his mind and fell back in line.

The other big bird was Horace. I called him that for Horace Greeley, the newspaper publisher of "Go west, young man" fame. Horace was the perfect turkey. Every feather was exactly in the right place, flawlessly colored a deep bronze brown that looked black from a distance. The other turkeys treated him with great respect. As a result, he had faultless manners. I never saw him peck or chase another bird in the flock.

Also, I noticed some of the hens seemed to act like mothers, leading the rest of the flock toward the grain when it was scattered for them to eat it. They also seemed to know when they should find places in the trees to roost.

Of course, I never told any of the others on the trail crew about those names and observations. They would have thought I was daft. But observing the different birds and comparing them with people helped me fill long, lonely hours of marching along with them.

Like myself, some of the turkeys got sore feet and began limping. Sometimes walking on the dry ruts of the wagon road injured their feet. Some birds got hurt by accidentally stepping on prickly pear cactus so they couldn't keep up. They were lucky. Rufus made a hospital for them in the small wagon. There, they were pampered patients and guests of honor, being served food and water as though they were staying in a four-star hotel or first-class passengers on a steamboat. But these thankless visitors were messy and smelly and crowded me out of my comfortable sleeping quarters for a few days, until there were more than fifteen "cripples."

I told Rufus those birds were smelling up the flour and beans that we were eating. Besides, they had almost filled up the space in the small wagon not occupied by food and kitchen items. So, the boss moved things around in the big wagon, transferred some sacks of grain to the small wagon and put the cripples in the big one.

After washing the wagon floor, I reclaimed my comfortable bedroom. I might be the lowest man on the totem pole on this drive, but at least I didn't sleep on the ground.

Late in the afternoon of the second day of our detour around the Grindstone Buttes, we were moving awfully slowly. Bill had drifted off to the right about two hundred yards. In fact, he was so far away I was worried about him. If someone should attack him out there, he'd be a goner for sure.

Ahead of him was a tiny stand of scrubby trees, totally leafless, that had grown up in a low spot on the prairie. There were two dark mounds off to one side of the trees, nestled in tall grass. One was twice as large as the other. *Maybe a couple of big rocks or a buffalo lying down with a calf.*

Bill saw them, too, and pushed his mule into a lope to investigate. Up close, he swung his mount around with a whoop and came back to the wagons at a full gallop, screeching as he came.

The instant he got to the big wagon, he scrambled inside

and shut the canvas cover behind him. I could hear his pitiful wailing, a mix between a groan and a whine.

Rufus yelled at him to find out what was wrong, but he couldn't get anything out of Bill. Then the boss hollered—cussing all the while—for one of the Johnson brothers to investigate.

The younger one galloped his horse to the small thicket, circled around it, and came back full tilt to the big wagon. He said the larger dark mound was a dead mule, the smaller a dead donkey. Nearby were three corpses, white men that had been killed, scalped, and stripped of their clothes.

Only when Rufus went to see the horrible sight did we realize that the victims were Joe Doaks, Joe Jones, and Joe Black—the Three Fugitives from our crew. Shocked by what he had seen, Rufus came puffing back and grunted orders to move the flock over the next ridge. He put Mr. Johnson up on the big wagon and one of the Johnson brothers rode with the flock and me. The other brother went with Rufus to bury the dead.

I was grateful for not having to see the bodies and not having to go near them. Rufus himself took care of the burial, which surprised me. Maybe he blamed himself for their deaths.

At supper, we all ate together in silence. No one asked what had happened. We all assumed a party of Cheyenne or Sioux had discovered the three white men and attacked. I don't know whether there were signs of a fight; I didn't want to know.

We all worried about what would happen next. Rufus guessed the attack had taken place three or four days earlier and that those responsible were far away by now, taking with them the low quality horse, pistols, and whatever property the three had worth taking. So, the threat of our being attacked wasn't exactly pressing. None of us wanted to end up like the Joes. We didn't say so, though. It struck me odd, too, that this company of men didn't talk about the incident, guessing this, speculating that, wondering how, when, and dozens of other details. Back home, unexplained deaths were grist for hours of discussion and gossip, even by the most uninformed.

Bill was still whimpering inside the canvas top of the big wagon. Rufus had taken him a plate of food and coffee, but he never touched it. Hearing a grown man weep is a hard thing to endure. His anguish was so sharp it stabbed all of us, making us wish we could make it go away. But we couldn't.

Never in my life had I felt so sad, so alone, so helpless. I was so far from home, from family, and from being safe. I don't know how I kept myself from crying. Busying myself with mealtime chores distracted me. But going to bed was the worst. Then the thoughts would pour in on me, drown me in a murky brew of dark feelings.

As I put away the pans and plates after washing them, I remembered how Zeb had brightened the evening with his stories of the past and his views of the current state of society. How I missed that old man. Almost as much as I missed my own parents. And my sister, Lucinda. Day by day—I hoped—I was getting closer and closer to seeing her again. But was it worth it?

Maybe I should have stayed at Uncle Asa's. It had been weeks since I seriously thought about that stingy old miser. He probably had more money than I'd ever have. But what good did it do him? He scrimped and scrounged, pinching every penny as hard as he could, living like a beggar. He certainly couldn't have gotten much pleasure from being so miserly.

Did he ever think of me? Probably not. But Aunt Clara would. Poor Aunt Clara. Uncle Asa had ground her down like a delicate tool, wearing her thin till there was hardly anything left. He treated her worse than he did his poorest hogs. But in her own way, she could be just as stubborn as he. She would never admit that.

That's when I decided I must write to Aunt Clara and tell her about my adventures. And to tell her I was sorry if my leaving had made her worry. I'd make a big point of never mentioning Uncle Asa or directing any of my message to his attention. But then what if he kept her from seeing my letter? He might, of course.

In my mind, I composed that letter. I had no paper, no pen, no lamp, or desk to write at, but in a short time everything I wanted to tell her was clear in my mind. Then I remembered the letter Joe Doaks had given me to mail. I would send it, of course. But I also had to write to his family to tell them what had happened to him.

For the next four days, Bill continued to hide in the big wagon. Sometime during the second day, he quit whimpering. Rufus said he drank a little water, but ate nothing. As thin and frail as Bill was, I worried that he might die, too.

Finding the remains of the Three Fugitives had a sobering effect on Rufus. Most of the time he was quiet, almost sullen. When he spoke, it was in a low, tired voice.

For a while, I thought his usual meanness was gone. But not for long.

"Ah been thinkin' about your sister," he said to me at breakfast the first morning after we had gotten back on the wagon road. "She's up there in Deadwood, havin' a high time—"

That was all I could take. I grabbed a bucket of cold water that I planned to heat for washing the dishes and threw it in Rufus's face. Then I let him have a furious torrent of all the nasty, foul words he had used on us, the oxen, the turkeys, the weather, the road, and everything else. I told him I had had enough of his bullying everyone, his disgusting language, his constant complaining, and his stupid drinking. I yelled that he had driven Zeb, John Blood, Eagle, and the three Joes out of camp and it was his fault four of them were dead now.

Finally, I screamed, "I quit!" and stalked out of camp.

Rufus was speechless for longer than I thought possible. By the time he began yelling, I was hundred yards up the road. Then I started running. And crying.

Chapter 12
Shadows

In my anger with Rufus Peach, I had jumped out of the frying pan into the fire. Nothing could have been dumber than stomping out of camp by myself in this hostile territory. But my wrath had been growing for weeks and he had finally delivered one insult too many.

As I stomped away from camp, I hoped that John Blood and Eagle Screams were still watching from a distance and would come riding on their wonderful ponies to rescue me from the mess I was in. But down deep, I knew they wouldn't come. They had said goodbye last night and were probably many miles away by now. I also expected Rufus to send a rider after me to haul me back to the fold like a belligerent runaway. I was fully a mile away from the camp when I stopped and looked back.

Habit told me the crew was busy taking down the wire pen, yoking up the bull team, saddling the horses and in general making ready for the morning's drive. I climbed up a small knoll and watched them. By now I felt foolish for my outburst. Remembering the surprised look on Rufus's face made me laugh a little, too. *Serves him right for all the crude things he's said to me.* No one had ever gotten the best of him before, so he would probably try to punish me. If he dared touch me, I'd leave for good, no matter how dangerous it was.

I could see the long rows of brown and white bulls pulling the tandem wagons. Spread out behind them like a strange dark blot on the prairie came the turkeys. Mr. Johnson's wagon followed the birds. It took them more than an hour to reach the foot of the knoll where I was sitting.

One of the Johnson brothers rode his horse up the slope and stopped in front of me. "Mr. Peach requests the honor of your presence at his wagon," he said, acting the smart-aleck.

"I've said all I have to say to that man," I snorted.

"And a right pert mouthful at that," he said, grinning. "So what should I tell him?" He sat, waiting.

I had to think about that. "He'll want to break my neck."

"Wull, you asked for it. But you're just a kid, so he might show a little mercy."

Now I noticed that Rufus had halted the bulls and the turkeys were being kept in place. I could see the boss staring at me a hundred yards away. Obviously, I was holding things up.

I got to my feet and walked slowly down the hill. The Johnson brother rode back to the flock. When I reached the big wagon, I looked up at Rufus, high on the wagon.

He looked so huge, ugly, and mean I wished that I had stayed up on that hill by myself.

"Get up here!" he ordered, sliding over on the seat to make room for me.

I crawled up beside him. With a wide swing of his arm, he lashed out with his whip, making it pop like a big pistol. The bulls pushed into their yokes and the wagon began to creak forward. I could see the front of Rufus's dirty shirt was all wet with the water I had thrown on him.

"I don't take kindly to sassin'," he began quietly. "My daddy used to whup us boys for back talk. Sometimes he hurt us real bad. Sometimes how he done was wrong. He always said it was for our own good." He fished into his pants pocket for a plug of tobacco and bit off a chunk. After working his jaw a few times, he spat a fine stream. "I ain't soft. I try to be fair. And I won't say nothin' more about your sister."

He chewed for a while and spat a couple of times. Then he scratched his belly. I had never sat so close to the man before, but now I noticed how much he needed to take a bath, especially the rank smell.

"I'll let bygones be bygones if you will," he said, offering his big paw-like hand.

"Yessir. I apologize for losing my temper." With that, I took his hand and shook it briefly.

He stopped the team of bulls and waited for me to climb down. As soon as my feet hit the ground, he whipped the huge animals into motion again. My ride on the big wagon had lasted only a minute or so during which we traveled fifty yards at most.

None of the men ever said anything about my dousing Rufus, but whenever they looked at me, they were trying to hide a smile. Most amazing about that morning's clash was that Rufus never swore at me again. That wasn't so for the others, though.

The next day we reached the stage stop where the Johnsons lived. A young man and his uncle with gold fever were there, waiting to join a larger party for safety on the road. Hearing about the massacre of the Three Fugitives shook them visibly, but Rufus assured them that we could protect ourselves. The uncle was a Mr. Brady and the nephew called himself Matthew Forbes. They were from Boston, soft city men who were out of place on the plains. Although they had been traveling horseback for weeks, the sallow paleness of city living still showed through the tans on their hands and faces. Both of them wore thick-lensed spectacles that made them look like grannies.

After four days of hiding in the big wagon, Bill came out. He seemed a little shakier than before. His view was still lost in the distance, his mind far away. Even so, when riding his mule, he sat as stiff and upright as a ramrod, with a true military bearing.

An hour into the morning's drive, I began to have the uneasy feeling of being watched. Sometimes in the distance I saw tiny movements on the horizon or hillsides that I couldn't explain. Once, I saw a rider on a horse and for a moment thought it might be John Blood, which made my heart jump. Then I remembered his pony was solid black, not spotted black and white.

When we stopped to graze the bulls and the turkeys,

the others said they had seen movements far off, too. Tension was rising. So far no one was outright frightened, but uneasy. Even Bill, in his blank state of mind, rode close to the flock, never wandering as he had a few days earlier.

Rufus took the Bostonians for a short walk, preaching to them the need to get out their firearms and be ready for combat. When they came back from their stroll, the poor city men were wide-eyed with fear. They got out a rifle and a double-barreled shotgun from one of their packs. Carrying the weapons was very awkward for them as they never found a way to hold them comfortably.

This time, if Rufus asked me to carry a gun, I'd gladly take it. The idea of killing someone was still unthinkable, but maybe shooting in the direction of attackers would discourage them. When the boss finished hitching up the bulls for the afternoon drive, I asked him for the pistol he had tried to force on me earlier. It was a .44 Navy Colt with a long barrel and, as I had expected, it weighed a half-ton. I slid it under my belt so the barrel pointed at the ground off to my left side and behind me.

We had gone another mile or so when I saw two riders stop on top a hill a quarter-mile away. They watched for a minute before they dropped out of sight. *This is getting too scary.*

Soon after that, a wagon pulled by a team of two horses came bumping over the crest of the road ahead of us, kicking up a small cloud of dust. With the wagon were two riders. They pulled up beside Rufus and shouted that a small party had been shot at up the road a few miles, but no one was hurt.

As it turned out, the four were buffalo hunters, searching for a large herd. The great herds on the southern plains had been "harvested," they said, so they were looking for a new start. When they saw our turkeys, they laughed and laughed. Tired of it, Rufus cut off their hilarity with a blast of his own saltiness.

Somehow, the boss hired the four hunters as guards for our drive. It was clear that they would have nothing to do with driving the birds. Their only job was to repel any attackers.

Like the Three Fugitives, the Four Buffalo Hunters kept their own company and were above talking to the rest of us. They all had fake names, one calling himself Robert Lee Winchester, another Jefferson Davis Colt, Stonewall Sharps and Alexander Stephens Springfield, surnames obviously borrowed from famous makes of firearms. They were even dirtier and smellier than Rufus. The sleeves of their shirts and coats were crusted with grime and grease from skinning buffalo. One of them wore a buckskin jacket stained with grease and dried blood. These were definitely not men you would introduce to your pretty sister.

The one thing they kept clean was their rifles. These were well-oiled, shiny instruments of death.

"Just so's I know you ain't a lot of hot air, I'd like to see if you can shoot," Rufus said.

This offended all four of them. For a moment, they looked like they might leave in a huff. Then the man who called himself Mr. Sharps admitted he was the poorest shot in the bunch, but he'd be glad to show what he could do. He went to their wagon, brought back his rifle, loaded it, and sat on the ground. He put up a bipod to support the heavy barrel of his firearm, fussed with the sights for a bit, and then carefully took aim at a rock five hundred yards away. The big weapon bellowed. We watched. And waited. Finally, a puff of dust rose behind the rock more than a quarter-mile away.

"Durn, I missed!" The other hunters laughed scornfully at him. Disgusted with himself, Mr. Sharps got up, went back to the wagon and put his rifle away.

As far as I could tell, if he had missed, it was only by an inch or two.

Rufus seemed satisfied with the new guards. He then gave the order to start the drive again.

For the first time in several days, I felt fairly safe, so I gave Rufus back the heavy revolver he had loaned me. Our crew was back up to nine men again, four of which we believed to be excellent riflemen. I had heard stories of the legendary marksmanship of buffalo hunters who could hit targets a half-mile away. They used large caliber rifles that launched heavy bullets that plowed through wind, brush, or anything else that got in the way. Once the bullet got there, it knocked down the object as though it had been hit by a speeding train.

It took only a short time to find out that I didn't like the Four Buffalo Hunters. I thought it would be interesting to hear about their experiences, but when they talked, it was only to each other.

For being unwashed drifters on the plains, they were incredibly snooty. They were almost as rude as the Johnsons, never directly answering a question from anyone except Rufus. In his case, they obligingly replied, as though they were doing him a big favor.

Mr. Winchester was tall, slim, well-built, and would have been handsome, given a good cleaning up, including a haircut and shave. He was probably in his late forties. His black hair had started to gray along the sides. He usually spoke with authority. He was the best shot and appeared to be the boss of the team.

Mr. Sharps was a large man with scruffy brown hair and an awesome paunch that hung over his wide leather belt like a sack of lukewarm slop. He was always belching and his clothes were usually unbuttoned, including his pants.

Mr. Colt was the youngest, probably in his twenties. He thought he was something special, bragging all the time about how much smarter than the others he was. He had been to some fancy college back east for a year and thought he knew the great secrets of the world, which he wouldn't share. He wore buckskin breeches with fringes down the seams on the outside. He had let his curly blond hair grow to shoulder length, apparently trying to look like Gen. George Armstrong Custer.

Mr. Springfield was the fourth buffalo hunter and the oldest. A bald-headed, short, runty little man, he had a high-pitched voice that whined most of the time. Sometimes he smoked a pipe and coughed and wheezed a lot afterward.

I figured that if there was a market for men, this foursome wouldn't bring much. They had no respect for people who had regular jobs and probably wouldn't do work that required using their hands and backs. Here they were getting paid to ride with us, carrying their guns, and that's all. They were our insurance—protection you hate paying for and hope you'll never actually need.

At night, Bill would linger by the campfire as I washed the dishes and put things away. He just stood around. If I handed him a towel, he became a motionless human towel rack. As always, he stared at something none of us could see.

Maybe Bill doesn't talk because no one talks to him. That thought came to me in an inspired moment. The only times I could remember anyone talking to Bill were during the poker game that day when we had laid over in the rain. The other time was when Rufus yelled at him after he had discovered the massacred Three Fugitives. That was no talking-to, of course. Bill was in no frame of mind to listen. The only times I had tried to talk to Bill were when I was joking around, trying to get a reaction out of him.

"Bill, did you like that stew we had tonight? That was made with antelope meat Mr. Springfield brought in this afternoon. I thought was pretty good, didn't you?"

Nothing.

"We've all seen Indians today. It's like they're playing cat and mouse with us. Did you see any?"

Nothing.

Then I talked about the turkeys, how most of the cripples had recovered and were carrying their own weight again. I told him about John Blood and Eagle coming to see me, leaving me Zeb's buffalo robe. I asked about his mule.

Still no sign he heard or understood me. I took the dry dish towel back. He had been holding it over his forearm as though he were a butler awaiting instructions. I put it away and started to go to the small wagon.

Bill was looking right at me. His eyes met mine for a full second during which he seemed to know me and then shifted away. Silently, he turned and left.

"Goodnight, Bill," I called.

Nothing.

The next day, the road took us up a pretty little valley with some evergreen trees in it. The hills on either side were taller and closer than we had been through since leaving Fort Pierre. We were a hundred yards from the head of the valley when two mounted Indians appeared on the crest of the hill. One of them pulled up a rifle and shot at us. The bullet flew over with an eerie buzz.

An instant later, one of the buffalo rifles roared in reply. One of the Indian ponies crumpled in his tracks. In a flash, the other horse, now carrying both warriors, vanished behind the top of the hill.

I had the sinking feeling that those shots were the beginning of a war for us.

Chapter 13
CLEANLINESS

That night we camped on the edge of a flat plain where we could see for miles in every direction. The buffalo hunters said they'd take turns keeping a night watch. All of us were pretty jumpy from being shot at earlier in the day.

The hunter who called himself Jefferson Colt asked me how old I was at supper and I told him I'd be fourteen in December.

"Thirteen? You mean to say you're only thirteen? You're awful big for thirteen. You sure you ain't fifteen or sixteen?"

It was true that I could look down on the short bantam-weight hunter, Mr. Sharps. The last year I was in school, I was the tallest boy in my class, but there were others who were stronger and could run faster.

"What are you doin' out here?" he asked loudly. "You runnin' away from home?"

I didn't like his attitude. And I didn't want to answer his questions because he would make a joke of anything he learned about me. So I decided to ignore him and his bad manners. I went back work, stirring batter for cornbread.

"Boy! Don't turn your back on me! I asked you a question!" He stepped up behind me, grabbed my shoulder and spun me around. Gripping the front of my jacket, he pulled me into his face.

"Let go," I said, a little scared.

Appearing in the nick of time, Rufus seized one of Mr. Colt's arms and jerked him around as though he were a rag doll. The young hunter let out a painful yelp.

"You ain't paid to pick on the cook," Rufus said coldly. "Just leave 'im be."

The Bostonians were watching through their eye-magnifying peepers in horror. The other buffalo hunters began laughing loudly. Put out by what had happened, Mr. Colt stalked off to the hunters' wagon to sulk, I figured. One thing was sure: Rufus had a new enemy.

By now my dislike for the buffalo hunters was strong. Although they were closed-mouthed about their own private matters, their strong Southern accent suggested they had all been soldiers in the Confederate Army. Rufus—who came from Missouri—was the only other Southerner on the crew. Bill, of course, wore his faded Union army pants with yellow stripes on the legs that were in tatters and a once-dark blue coat that was nearly gray from fading and dust. The Bostonians kept still, so there was no telling where their sympathies were. But, being New Englanders, I assumed they had favored the

Union and maybe Mr. Brady had even fought for it.

Father once said that for many soldiers, the War Between the States would never end, no matter how many years passed. Hatred of the enemy for what they had done to each other would not permit them to forget and forgive, regardless of any surrender or reconstruction. Father had been an infantryman in the Illinois Seventy-sixth Regiment. The main thing he said about the war was that it was horrible.

I suspected the Four Buffalo Hunters still carried hard feelings, even though the war had ended twelve years earlier. Sometimes the others called Mr. Winchester "Colonel." Was it because he had been a colonel in the Confederate army or just because he was in charge of the four of them?

They had noticed Bill's threadbare uniform and commented to each other in low voices. I expected them to poke fun at Bill because he never spoke and rarely showed signs of listening. But they seemed to respect him, which I was glad to see.

Our procession changed with the new armed guards. One rode with Rufus in the big wagon, leading the drive. Another went on horseback, cradling his heavy rifle in his lap. The other two rode in their own wagon, behind the flock. All four constantly searched the horizon and nearer points for any sign of unwelcome visitors.

The hunter on horseback liked to rove, more or less circling the whole drive every hour or two. That bothered Bill, of course, who was used to doing the same thing himself. Not knowing quite what to do, he tried to stay across the flock from the mounted buffalo hunter.

Once I noticed that something had caught Bill's attention and he rode his mule a short distance to have a closer look. From there, he rode in a wide circle around the flock. His wandering made me nervous for two reasons. One, he wasn't protected when off by himself. And two, I was afraid he might stumble onto other victims left on the prairie.

Mid-morning came and we paused to graze the bulls and give the turkeys a little corn. The mounted buffalo hunter just then was Mr. Springfield, who said he'd ride ahead to scout the road. Just before we began moving again, he returned and reported he had seen riders off to the northwest. He judged them to be Indians of some kind. That news brought a torrent of cussing from Rufus, but he gave the order to move ahead, anyway.

By now the day had turned pleasantly sunny and too warm for winter clothes. I had pealed off my jacket when we stopped earlier and stowed it in the small wagon. The turkeys lolled along slowly.

The big turkey I called Buzzard had singled out a scrawny bird to pick on and kept chasing it around through the flock. Watching this distracted me for perhaps a half hour. The next time I looked around, I saw that Bill was gone.

"Hey, where's Bill?" I shouted.

"Who?" the older Bostonian asked.

"Bill, the old soldier. He's gone."

Word was passed quickly to the big wagon. Rufus called a halt and berated us for not watching better. He was frantic. Right away, he barked at two buffalo hunters to go out in different directions to find the missing drover.

Instantly and loudly, they refused.

Rufus then turned to the Bostonians. From the look on his face, you could see he knew it was pointless to ask them to risk searching the prairie. They'd probably get lost themselves.

Now Rufus seemed completely helpless, confused, panicky. This great, blustering hulk of a man had suddenly turned into a big, fumbling child.

"Get me a horse and *I'll* find him," I said. "He can't be far."

The buffalo hunters scoffed at my offer, saying I'd be crazy to go.

"I'd go with you, but..." Mr. Brady, the uncle, made the excuse that his spine troubled him after riding hard. However, he said I could ride his horse if I wanted to.

"I don't know," Rufus said in a troubled voice.

Standing around fretting wasn't helping Bill any. I took the reins of Mr. Brady's horse, mounted, and rode back down the trail, trying to remember where we were exactly when Bill wandered out to look at something in the distance. Off to the left, I saw a dark object that turned out to be a low bush. In the grass I could see the faint tracks of a large animal, which I guessed was Bill's mule. They led up a low rise and into a shallow draw beyond. At the upper end of the draw was a small thicket of junipers.

Going there meant exposing myself to a possible ambush, if hostiles were hiding there. The horse I had was old and in bad shape, so there'd be no escape.

But if Bill was in that thicket and I didn't bring him back, I might be to blame for his being lost forever.

Nervously, I prodded the old gelding into a trot toward the small grove of evergreens. As I got closer, a movement in the trees gave me a sudden start. I slowed the horse to a walk, watching the trees with wide eyes. At the last moment, I saw that the animal was Bill's mule, tied to a dead branch of one of the junipers.

Dismounting, I tiptoed forward to see what Bill was doing. Was I surprised when I found him sitting in a shallow pool of water, taking a bath! A spring bubbled out of the head of the draw, providing moisture for the small bunch of trees that formed a perfect screen for bathing. It was strange to see skinny old Bill sitting in a few inches of water. His hands and face were tanned a rich brown, but all the rest of him was as pale as swiss cheese.

"Bill!" I yelled.

He jumped about a mile and plopped back down in the water with a splash. Instantly, his face turned bright red. Even the back of his neck blushed.

"Rufus was scared you got waylaid. Finish up quick and let's get out of here." I went back to Mr. Brady's horse and waited.

In a couple of minutes, Bill came out, buttoning up his old coat. Riding at a lope, it took us almost a half-hour to get back to the drive.

Rufus had regained his bluster and was fuming about lost time when we arrived. Again, he cussed out the turkeys for bringing him such misery and ordered us to move on. His behavior sure was confusing. One moment he was paralyzed with fear and worry about Bill; the next he acted like he didn't care about the old soldier. Rufus never asked where I found him, what he was doing, or anything. And, of course, he never thanked me, either.

That night, after supper, the boss came back to the fire to refill his coffee cup and sheepishly poured in a dollop of whiskey, without saying a word to me. He was starting to waddle back to the big wagon when I asked him to stay and talk to me.

"Yeah, whatta ya want?" He slurped up a mouthful of coffee and swallowed it with a froggy sound.

"I want to know about Bill."

"He ain't your business."

"*He is, too*," I said impatiently. "I was the only one who would go look for him. I deserve to know something about him."

Rufus stared at the fire for a long time. "Wull, mebbe you do."

Anger came into his eyes, enough to scare me a little.

"Bill is my brother, William Washington Peach. When we were boys, he was our great hope. He was to be the lawyer, our brother Ned the doctor, and me the dentist."

That was a laugh—Rufus Peach yanking out people's teeth? And terrifying children and lady patients with his rowdy cussing? But the sad sound of his voice stilled any snicker I might have had.

"Bill was readin' the law with an attorney in Springfield. When he got to lawyerin', he was going to put Ned and me through college. Then the war came. Missouri was a slave state, but we were poor and never had any slaves, never believed it was right. So Bill went up to Iowa and joined a cavalry outfit. By the time he was twenty-three, they made him a major. He was a great soldier."

This part was really hard for Rufus to tell.

"In '64 he was being transferred to a different company. A bunch of Rebs captured him on the road and he spent the rest of the war in a Confederate prison in Alabama. He got the malaria there, but it couldn't kill him.

"When Union forces opened that prison, they put most of the men on the steamboat *Sultana* to get them home as fast as they could. Well, they were pushing that ol' boat too hard and she blew up just above Memphis. Killed more than eighteen hundred men."

Rufus sat silent for a long time.

"It blew up Bill's mind, too. He ain't never said a word in twelve years since. Sometimes I wish—for his sake—it had took him, too. Instead of leaving him nothin' but a shadow of a man." By now, Rufus's eyes were red and watery.

"And you've taken care of him all that time?"

"Naw. He lived with Ned on the farm until a couple of years ago. Then Ned died of the cholera and his wife sold the farm. That's when I took Bill. All our big plans just dried up." He tossed down the rest of his coffee, wiped his nose with the back of his hand, and went back to the big wagon.

Rufus didn't tell me to keep the story of Bill to myself, but that seemed best. Just when I thought Rufus was a hopeless bully, I saw that he did have a heart. And that caring for his invalid brother put a great burden on him.

At breakfast the next morning, Jefferson Colt, the young buffalo hunter with such a high opinion of himself, teased me about having to walk all the time.

"I don't have a horse."

"Don't sass me!" he growled.

I wasn't trying to be fresh. I had simply stated the obvious. "I don't have money for a horse right now," I retorted.

"Leave the kid alone," Mr. Winchester, the boss buffalo hunter ordered. "After all, he's the one that brought back the dummy."

Rufus was just finishing his food when the hunter made that remark. Furious, he hurled his tin plate to the ground. He glared a hole in the back of Mr. Winchester's shirt, but the hunter never knew it. After a moment, Rufus picked up his plate. I think he would have walloped Mr. Winchester, but he knew the other buffalo hunters would join the fracas and the rest of us wouldn't. So, he thought better of it. To hide the scowl on his face, Rufus turned away and went to yoke the bulls. If someone made another crack like that, I was sure he wouldn't let it go.

Chapter 14
CROSSING THE RIVER

For the next few days, we crawled across the flat prairie, going straight west along the wagon road, meeting no other travelers. Some days it was windy, but the weather was fairly warm by mid-morning.

The Four Buffalo Hunters avoided the rest of us except at mealtime. That was fine with me. But the youngest, Mr. Colt, kept taunting me whenever he had the chance. I don't think he meant to be particularly mean. He just thought his razzing me was funny. One morning he asked how old I was when I left home. At first, I ignored the question, but when he started to get ugly about it, I told him, "I left a few months ago."

"I was seven when my pappy threw me out," he boasted. "I joined the Army of the C. S. A. when I was eight. Them was hard years."

"So you were in the war," I said, inviting him to go on.

He gave me a dirty look, shook his head as if to say "How could you ask such a stupid question?" and walked away.

A couple of times I tried to talk to Mr. Brady and his nephew, Mr. Forbes, but they treated me like some kind of intruder. They both wore mismatched parts from old suits, now threadbare and baggy. I figured they must have had some kind of office jobs in Boston. Neither of them cared to talk to anyone else, so we left them alone.

Except for complaining about the food, no one talked to me, either. So this was the loneliest part of the trip. I kept on talking to Bill, but that was hopeless because he never replied.

Rising early, cooking breakfast, driving turkeys, cooking supper, and packing up the kitchen filled my days, but the nights were awful. Usually, I'd fall asleep soon after turning in because I was worn out, but in the middle of the night, I'd wake up and think about how terribly I missed Mother and Father, how lonely it was without being able to talk to my sister Lucinda or my good school friends in Kankakee. In those black hours of the night, I felt so bad that I sat up and let the tears run down my cheeks, but kept from crying out loud.

Why is there so much pain? Why me? It's so unfair. Then one night I realized I wasn't the only one who was feeling hurt. Rufus, poor old Bill, and thousands of others who had suffered through the war—including cocky young Mr. Colt—had lots of pain, too.

Zebulon Smith had told me that out here you need a partner. He was right, of course. But on top of that, I knew that you need a family, too. I realized I would always need my family, even if only my sister was left.

Lucinda, you just have to be there when I get to Deadwood. If you're not, I don't know what I'll do.

One morning Rufus announced that we would get to the Cheyenne River by evening and cross over the next day. He said it was usually a rough crossing because of the high river banks.

That puzzled me. I couldn't see any sign of a river from where we were. The land was almost flat, gently rolling off in the distance. By mid-day, though, the land between us and the horizon had opened up to reveal a rugged, broken bluff on the far side of a valley, mottled with junipers. So far, there was no sign of the bluff on this side of the valley and certainly no telling how deep it was. Such a drastic change in terrain was exciting after weeks of rolling, mostly treeless plains.

After breakfast, Rufus waited until we were alone, came up close to me, and whispered: "Take this and keep it out of sight." He handed me a derringer, a tiny two-barreled pistol, that I could hide in my hand.

"Our buffalo-huntin' guards have been acting mighty peculiar the past couple of days," he explained. "This is just in case they try to pull something unfriendly." A moment later, he climbed up on the big wagon and started the bull team with a crack of his whip and a couple dozen of his choicest words.

At first, I put the derringer in my pants pocket, but it was so heavy it showed. Putting it in my jacket pocket worked better. The fact that Rufus trusted me enough to confide in me gave me a new feeling of importance. But he really didn't have any other choice.

At midday, as we were eating our cold lunch, Mr. Winchester was most somber as he told us, "Keep yo' eyes open for trouble. So fah we haven't seen any raidskins, but I can feel 'em out there."

Well, he and the other buffalo hunters had been saying alarming things like that for three days. I guessed they talked like that to make Rufus believe they were earning their pay.

Besides, a big bank of thick, dark clouds was gathering on the horizon to the northwest. *No Indian would attack in bad weather*, I told myself as if I really knew. Rufus, too, saw the clouds. The more he looked at them, the more worried he became, muttering and swearing at length.

At mid-afternoon, we reached the edge of the bluffs on the eastern side of the Cheyenne River. The valley below was beautiful, deep and rugged, even under the darkening sky and rising wind. Most days we stopped at this hour to set up camp for the night. But Rufus said we'd push on to the river.

Wending our way down the bluff was difficult and slow. We followed a sloping ridge that had deep ravines on either side. Battered by the wind, the birds wanted to flee into the gullies and trees. It took at lot of work to keep them on track.

Then one of hunters yelled a warning and pointed to the bluff behind us. I couldn't see what he was hollering about, but I didn't like it. The other hunters held their rifles at the ready and scoured the hills with eagle eyes.

When we reached the narrow flat at the bottom of the valley, large drops of rain began to splatter down.

Predictably, Rufus swore a blue streak at the storm. He said we had to cross the river right now. A big rain would make the stream rise and we'd be in danger if we camped there, caught between a rampaging river and bluffs that would protect anyone who attacked us.

First, we penned the turkeys. Then Rufus took the wagons and the Bostonians across the river to unload the cargo. Then they came back and put as many of the birds as they could into both wagons. Rufus ordered the buffalo hunters to haul birds in their wagon, too, but they refused. The look Rufus gave them would have made the devil shiver, but it didn't faze those hunters.

Mr. Winchester did ride in the big wagon with Rufus, though, doing his job as guard. The other hunters and I stayed with the penned turkeys and watched as the bulls patiently pulled the wagons through the muddy river, about knee deep. On the far side, they set up a small pen for the birds, unloaded and returned. That first load had only seventy birds in it.

The rain beat down harder and harder. Soon we were soaked to the skin and shaking from the cold. Again, we caught and loaded turkeys as fast as we could without hurting the birds. When the wagons were full, Rufus roared through the rain, "Throw in some more!" So we added another thirty. I was afraid they would smother, piled up as they were.

The wagons had just entered the water when shots rang out from the bluffs behind us. In the pouring rain, it was impossible to see where the bullets were hitting. The buffalo hunters, Messrs. Colt, Springfield, and Sharps, couldn't see any clear targets. But every once in a while one of them would aim at the bluffs and blast away, hoping to discourage the attackers there. It didn't.

By the time the wagons had pulled out of the river to unload, the turkeys in the pen had panicked from the gunshots and the thunderstorm and flew out of the enclosure and found refuge in some large cottonwood trees. Rufus screamed something about the turkeys flying back across the river, but luckily, they just moved farther away as newly-arrived birds joined them.

The next trip, we piled in even more turkeys and Rufus whipped the bulls back into the rising river. For the first time, the bulls began struggling and acting unruly. The river was now running about three feet deep.

I think Rufus had planned to make two more trips to finish the crossing, but the rising water, the driving rain and occasional shots pushed him into taking the rest on the fourth trip.

Turkeys were about three layers deep in the wagons. Rufus insisted the buffalo hunters take part of the wire pen in their wagon on this final crossing. This time, they agreed and even helped lift the rolls into the wagon box.

Now the shooting from the bluffs increased. Every once in a while a bullet flew by with a whine or buzz. But so far, no one had been hit. Two of the hunters, Messrs. Winchester and Colt, returned as much fire as they could from the wagons in which they were riding. I was in the small wagon, up to my neck in wet turkeys that were climbing all over each other for a breath of air.

At midstream, water pushed against the sides of the wagon box and leaked in under the tailgate. Clearly, the river was rising and threatening to carry us away.

Shooting from the bluffs increased again and a dozen riders galloped up to the riverbank, stopped, and fired at us from close range. Some of them were dressed up like Indians, but I could see we were being attacked by a gang of road agents. Now the hunters made every shot count. Only two of the nearby robbers escaped alive.

Bullets ripped through the canvas cover of the small wagon and into the wagon box. I just prayed we wouldn't be hit.

Mr. Sharps, the short, bald-headed buffalo hunter, was the only one in our party still on horseback. He was riding to the right, downstream, of the rear wagon, fighting to control his horse in the swift water. Suddenly, he jerked back in pain and dropped his rifle into the river. Slowly, he sagged forward and slipped off his horse into the muddy water. Then he was gone. The horse bolted, struggling to get to the far shore.

It took forever to get to the west bank of the river, even though the stream was only fifty yards wide. As we crept away, the robbers' fire thinned out. The hunters' deadly shooting had driven them back. I was beginning to believe we would make it.

The big wagon was completely out of the water when the right front wheel on the little wagon broke with a loud crack, dropping that corner into the water. At the same instant, the tongue broke out of the little wagon, so we began drifting downstream.

The hunters' light wagon came around us and bumped up onto the shore. Mr. Colt threw me a rope from the bank. I quickly tied my end around the front axle. He fastened the other end to the back of the hunters' light wagon, preventing our floating away.

I was alone in the small wagon with sixty turkeys. We were only a few feet from shore, so I knew I could jump off and wade to land. But Mr. Colt kept yelling at me to stay with the wagon.

Slowly, Rufus came back with the bull team and a heavy chain to pull us out of the raging water. After hooking up and trying, it was clear that the wagon would tip over because the remaining good front wheel was cocked at the wrong angle.

"We're gonna have to carry them off!" Rufus shouted through the rain.

Moments later, we had a human chain passing turkeys from the wagon to shore like a fireman's bucket brigade. When the final bird was unloaded, I jumped out of the wagon. Hanging on to the rope that secured it, I waded to the riverbank.

Now Rufus started the bulls. Almost instantly, the wagon rolled over on its side and was dragged that way up onto the gravel bank. Then he was able to tip it upright and pull it up onto higher ground for repairs. The rain turned into a fine drizzle as darkness came. The road agents across the river had pulled out. I worried that more robbers or an Indian war party was waiting for us in the bluffs ahead of us.

Everything was a mess. The downpour had soaked the cargo from the wagons. The grain for the turkeys was wet, as was our clothing, the flour, beans, cornmeal, salt pork, clothing, and bedding. All of us—including the turkeys, now safely roosting in the trees around us— looked like grumpy wet hens.

First, we set up the tarpaulin shelter so we could work out of the misty rain. The Bostonians gathered wood from along the river and before long, we had a crackling fire going, welcome relief from the chilly evening.

By the time it was dark, I had a supper of cornbread, venison stew, and hot coffee ready. No one had much to say. Mr. Sharps had died in the river and was washed away; his partners avoided talking about him. No one felt very good, that's for sure. But we didn't grumble. We could have been in far worse shape.

During the night, the fine rain turned to snow for a while before the sky cleared. In the morning, the Cheyenne River valley was magnificent in a light, angelic coat of white that glistened in the sunlight. Rufus said we'd lay over for a day or two to dry out and to fix the broken wheel on the small wagon. Then he ordered us to spread out some of the wet grain from the wagon to feed the turkeys. In a short while, they all winged their way down from the trees and were feeding hungrily.

By mid-morning, the snow had melted and the sun began drying our things. Rufus spread the covers from the wagons on the grass and then poured out the rest of the wet grain to dry on them. We had clothes and blankets hanging from all the nearby trees, too.

With surprising skill, Rufus cut wood from a green ash tree and rebuilt the wheel so you could hardly tell it had been broken. And he did it all with just a few hand tools and a small fire.

Late in the afternoon, we put up the wire pen for the birds and lured them into it with a few buckets of corn.

By the end of the day, our skins and souls had dried

out and our spirits were rising again. We expected to start again early the next morning. Messrs. Winchester and Colt had scouted ahead and returned with good news: No sign of robbers or Indians.

At supper, we all ate together again. Somehow getting through the crisis of crossing the river bound us together. I was beginning to think that despite their rough edges, these men were all right.

Then it happened. Mr. Winchester pulled a big pistol out of his pants and stuck the barrel against the side of Rufus's head.

"Gennulmen, ah regret to infawm you we ah takin' chawge of this here outfit. Make any hint of trouble and you *will* die."

Messrs. Colt and Springfield quickly searched us for weapons. They took a pocket knife away from young Mr. Forbes of Boston. Bill's big "U.S." holster was empty. Rufus had a Barlow knife they took away. Luckily for me—I guess—I had hung my jacket on a tree to dry with the derringer still in the pocket, so I was clean.

I could just see the cuss words squeezing out every pore on Rufus's body, he was so angry. But he kept his peace. For now.

Chapter 15
AFOOT

Being held prisoners by the buffalo hunters was no picnic. The first night they herded us—Rufus, Bill, Mr. Brady, Mr. Forbes, and myself—into the small wagon to sleep. They let us have our blankets and my buffalo robe, but when we all tried to lie down on the floor of the wagon, we bumped into each other all the time.

The air wasn't very good, either. Bill was the only one in the wagon who had had a bath in a month, so the body odors were bad, especially the stench of unwashed feet.

Finally, two of the men went to sleep and began a snoring contest. Neither of them was Rufus because after a while, I heard him cuss them out, but got no response. So he gave each of them a kick hard enough to wake them so they muttered about being poked.

That gave Rufus a chance to drop off to sleep and start

snoring himself, louder than either of the other two. Of course, no one had nerve enough to kick him.

I was just getting to sleep when one of the men got up and stepped on my face getting out of the wagon. The guard outside wanted to know where he was going. To meet nature's call, he said.

Twice again in the darkness, someone had to get up, stumbled over me, woke the guard, and made it almost impossible to go back to sleep. Before I knew it, they were rousting me out to make breakfast. I felt like I hadn't had one minute's rest all night.

Lucinda would laugh if she heard about this pickle, I told myself. *But she'd worry, too, about what the buffalo hunters are going to do with us.* That scared me, too.

Mr. Winchester gave a little speech at breakfast. First, he said no one would be permitted to ride a horse or mule. Rufus, of course, would drive the tandem wagon. The rest of us—Bill, Mr. Brady, Mr. Forbes, and myself— were to drive the turkeys on foot.

The horses and Bill's jenny would be haltered and led behind the hunters' wagon. If anyone tried to escape by walking off or attempted to take one of the mounts, they would be shot. Also, there would be no privacy. Anyone attempting to do anything out of sight of the hunters would be putting himself in the utmost danger.

"Are there any questions?"

We all refused to look at or talk to him.

"Fine. Now get to work."

Rufus went to hitch up the bulls. I cleaned up the kitchen goods and got them loaded into the small wagon. The Bostonians took down the wire pen for the turkeys and loaded it and the steel posts into the big wagon. Bill mostly stood and stared at the river behind us.

When Mr. Springfield started to halter Bill's mule, she tried to take a bite out of his shoulder, but he dodged away. He got a big stick to whack the jenny when Bill came up, slipped the halter over her ears and buckled it with ease. He handed Mr. Springfield the end of the lead rope and the mule lunged and got away. She trotted a few feet away and stopped to wait patiently for Bill.

Under other circumstances, this would have been funny. But Mr. Springfield was in such an ugly mood that if he were pushed any further, he'd probably put a bullet in the unruly jenny's head.

Climbing out of the Cheyenne River valley was almost as hard as descending into it. Trees, bushes, and little gullies offered the turkeys places to explore and to hunt for food. But now it was November 9 and at this higher elevation, other birds and animals had eaten the berries and the insects had long ago vanished for the season.

So we spent a lot of time chasing strayed bunches of turkeys. By mid-morning, we had mounted the rolling grasslands above the river, where trees were visible only in the ravines and along the creeks.

All of the men were complaining about being tired and having sore feet. In fact, Mr. Brady had several blisters on the heels of his feet where his boots had rubbed them. Bill limped along, saying nothing, but it was easy to see he wasn't enjoying the hike.

Only Mr. Forbes accepted being afoot with good humor. He told me that as a child he had been ordered to take a carriage everywhere he went. He once learned to ride a bicycle, but his mother said that was too dangerous, so she insisted he go only in carriages.

Discovering that he could actually walk long distances pleased him. On the way up the bluff, he found a good walking stick, helpful for climbing slopes and hurling at runaway turkeys.

While we rested, the three buffalo hunters huddled to talk in low voices, apparently planning our fate.

Rufus came over and whispered, "You still got that gun?"

"Yessir. It's in my jacket pocket."

"Keep it on you. When I give the nod, use it."

Before I could ask him what he meant, he had walked away. *Does he mean now, in the next minute or two? Later in the day? Tomorrow? Does he expect me to blast one of the buffalo hunters? What does Rufus want?*

In the afternoon, a stagecoach bound for Fort Pierre passed us. The driver and a passenger on top waved frantically as they went by. Obviously, they had no idea we were being held prisoners.

Maybe someone will come along and rescue us. But then we had believed the Four Buffalo Hunters had come along and saved us from the Indians and robbers! Now I recalled Rufus saying you couldn't trust the scum on the road. I just wished we had a plan for regaining control of the herd.

Late in the afternoon we stopped to make camp, turning the bulls and turkeys loose to graze. Our captors still watched us closely. They were suspicious of every move we made. Constantly, they were pointing their guns at us, bossing us around.

I told Mr. Winchester we were out of some supplies because of the rain and low on others that we needed. Moisture had ruined our sugar. The wheat flour was also a soggy mass which I didn't think I'd be able to use much longer.

He grumbled it wasn't his problem; talk to Mr. Peach. When I told him I would, he ordered me to stay away from the boss.

At supper time, Messrs. Winchester and Colt were quite jovial. They apparently had been thinking about all the money they'd get from selling the turkeys in Deadwood. However, Mr. Springfield was quiet, almost worried. As he should be.

Rufus rose to get a second cup of coffee and stepped behind Mr. Winchester. He nodded at me to get behind Mr. Colt, which I did, pretending to check on the cooking fire.

Rufus stuck his pistol in Mr. Winchester's ear and said loudly, "Ah regret to inform you we're takin' this outfit back *right now*." Mr. Winchester stiffened as if touched by an icicle.

I pushed the cold barrel of the derringer against the back of Mr. Colt's head, just under the ear.

"You ain't got guts enough to shoot me," Colt hissed over his shoulder.

I moved the little pistol a couple of inches and fired one barrel with a roar. Mr. Colt dropped his plate and begged me not to fire again.

Bill had silently pushed his huge six-shooter into Mr. Springfield's face. *Yes, Bill!* I couldn't believe it, but I was sure glad he had.

Rufus ordered Mr. Forbes to disarm the hunters of their pistols, knives, and rifles. He then made them lie on their backs on the ground, heads touching, and tied their wrists together so their arms formed a circle. While lashing them together, Rufus gave them a chewing like they had never heard before.

"You can't leave us like this all night," Mr. Winchester complained.

"Oh, we won't, *Colonel*. We're gonna stake your feet down, too, you old goat." Now Rufus had an immense grin on his face. Not being in control for the past day had been really hard on him. He came around and shook hands with all of us for rescuing the drive from this bunch of crooks.

Well, Lucinda, your worrying about us would have been a waste. I felt very good about regaining our freedom.

At dusk, a train of wagons drawn by bulls creaked up from the west. At first, Rufus was pleased to see company coming. But when he saw who they were, his pleasure wilted.

When the thirty-two wagons arrived, they circled our camp and hemmed us in. A burly driver jumped down from the lead wagon, swaggered over and said loudly, "Rufus, it's time you paid up."

"You know I can't do that right now," our boss said weakly. "Once I get these birds to Deadwood, I will. You know that."

"Boys, let's shoot the whole dadburned bunch!" one of the teamsters shouted.

"No!" Rufus screamed. "You can't do that!"

Forty men surrounded us with a fearsome collection

of firearms. I figured they could do anything they took a notion to. Then a quiet man in dark clothes and a derby hat pushed through from the rear and walked up to Rufus. It was Mr. Volin.

"Rufus, my drivers say you cheated them out of a thousand dollars playing poker in Pierre."

"Wull—" Rufus scratched the back of his neck and scuffed his boot in the dirt on the road. "I ain't no cheat. If they're gonna be such sore losers, I'll give 'em their dadburned money back. But right now it's all tied up in this drive."

We'll call it even if you just turn the turkeys over to us," Mr. Volin's wagon boss said.

Rufus replied with a blast of swear words that meant "No."

"Sir, those turkeys are rightfully ours," one of the teamsters called to the captain of the wagon train.

Mr. Volin said that if the birds were still in Fort Pierre, the teamsters might claim them. But now, two-thirds of the way to Deadwood, Mr. Peach and his company had invested much time and labor moving them. Besides, out here, their value had increased, too, the reward of Mr. Peach's industry and willingness to take some risk. "Let him finish the drive, sell the birds, and then pay you off."

A round of grumbling circulated among the teamsters. Then one piped up, "If they's our birds, we kin eat some, I say."

That set off a chorus of shouting and whistling. In the end, Rufus let them have five birds, their value to be subtracted from the thousand-dollar debt when paid off.

Two men went into the pen and selected the birds. I

couldn't watch them choose and had to walk away when they butchered them.

Mr. Volin stayed and talked to Rufus for a while. As before, Rufus said "yessir" a lot and made excuses about many of the things the freighter brought up. I eavesdropped while I was cleaning up after our meal.

"Where did you get the idea for this drive?" Mr. Volin asked.

"Wull... I don't remember... exactly."

"I have two younger brothers who plan to do this same thing next year. Do you know about their plans?"

"Uhn... I don't think so."

"Are you thinking of doing it again?"

"Oh, lordy, nossir! You can't imagine the trouble we've had on this trip. I ain't never trying nothin' like this again."

The conversation then turned to gossip about events along the road. Rufus told about our trouble crossing the Cheyenne—he said he thought it was the bandit gang from Robbers Roost—and being hijacked by the buffalo hunters. Mr. Volin mentioned a couple of raids on wagon trains and small parties of travelers farther west.

They came to terms on our prisoners, too. The wagon train would deliver the hunters to the U.S. Army detachment in Fort Pierre. From there, they would be sent to Yankton to face charges of attempted robbery. Rufus paid the hunters for their time and bought their rifles and ammunition.

As a favor, he said, Mr. Volin ordered two of his men to help us get to Deadwood. I suspect he also told them to watch Rufus to make sure the teamsters got their money back.

"Which two?" Rufus asked.

"Mendez and Olson," Mr. Volin said.

Rufus frowned. "How about someone else?"

"They'll do you a good job," Mr. Volin said firmly, closing the discussion.

The next morning the bull train hitched up and left while we were still eating breakfast. I was glad to see them go and even happier that they were taking the buffalo hunters with them.

The new men were named Luis Mendez and Hans Olson. They seemed to be friendly and have a good sense of humor, smiling about the razzing the other teamsters had given them for having to drive turkeys. They both rode beautiful, large chestnut geldings.

All morning as we went west at a snail's pace, I felt something was wrong. But what? When we stopped to graze at mid-morning, it finally came to me. Horace, the perfect turkey, and Buzzard, the big bully, were gone, eaten by Mr. Volin's teamsters.

Chapter 16

THE PROMISED LAND

For the next three days, Rufus crowed that we were "almost there," but it just looked like more of the same to me. We were still inching along the deep wagon tracks over the rolling, grassy prairie. As we went west, the hills seemed to gradually climb. Yet, we saw no mountains. Traffic on the road increased some. Once or twice a day, a stagecoach, wagon train, single wagon or small group of riders came along from either east or west. All these travelers found our flock of turkeys very funny.

By now, I was anxious to get to Deadwood. There was still some danger of hostiles or bandits attacking us.

One of the new drovers, Luis Mendez, liked to cook and began helping me at mealtime. He, too, told Rufus that we needed flour, sugar, and other supplies to make up for those we lost crossing the Cheyenne. Because he was no longer distracted by the Buffalo Hunters or because a grown man was speaking to him, Rufus agreed to send a party into Rapid City as soon as we got close enough.

Instantly, I got my hopes up, expecting to make that trip. I was beginning to wonder if there were any towns in this wilderness.

The next day dawned foggy and quiet. We traveled for an hour or so and had reached the crest of a low ridge when the wind came up and blew so hard the turkeys couldn't stay on their feet. For a bit, I thought they would be bowled over like tumbleweeds and go cartwheeling across the prairie and be lost. Seeing all the trouble the birds were having, the boss called a halt and said we'd lay over until the wind died down. Everyone on the crew was relieved not to be fighting the gale, but there was nowhere to hide from it or the chill it drove through you like icy spikes.

We penned the turkeys and gave them grain to eat. By the time we finished, the fog had lifted and the sun pierced the clouds above. To the south and west rose a light blue ribbon of mountains. The Black Hills, at last! We could see the promised land!

"Me 'n Josh can take this time to go into Rapid to get some extra grub," Mr. Mendez suggested to Rufus.

Peppering his reply with purple and blue words, the boss said it wasn't necessary for me to go along with Mr. Mendez.

"But Señor Peach, Josh is *the cook*. He has earned a leetle time off."

"Naw. Have him make up a list. You take Bill and go."

My spirits dropped through the soles of my shoes. *There*

they go again, treating me like a useless kid.

Mr. Mendez walked over to the little wagon with me and told me to make up the list of supplies. "You're coming along, too," he said. "You'll see." That didn't seem very likely since Mr. Mendez was about my size, not exactly someone to boss big Rufus around.

"How can you get him to change his mind?"

"Socks."

"Socks?"

"Sure," he said with a broad smile. "We tell heem you need new socks. Bill don't know what size you wear. And maybe you want cotton socks. Perhaps wool? And what color? See? *We don't know,*" he said with great helpless gesture. "So what we gonna do?"

I waited for his answer.

"We gotta take you along to make sure we get it right. Why, a pair of socks costs a dime out here in the territory. That's too much to take a chance on the wrong thing."

He can't be serious, I told myself with a smirk. Sometimes Rufus wasn't the brightest man in the world, but he would never fall for a line like that.

A moment later, Mr. Mendez strutted over to the boss and asked if he could have a moment of his time. They walked off a way, leaning into the wind to keep from tipping over. Mr. Mendez would say something that ended with a question and Rufus would nod "Yes." After about five minutes, Mr. Mendez came back, grinning.

"You can ride Hanson's horse," he announced.

Two minutes later, Bill, Mr. Mendez, and I were galloping south toward Rapid City.

In the few days I had known him, Mr. Mendez told me

about Mexico and Texas and his driving cattle to the railheads in Kansas. He taught me enough Spanish to greet people, to ask for meat and beans, and to say, "*Mi hermana es muy bonita.*" (My sister is very pretty.)

There was a sparkle in his eyes that made you like him instantly. He loved to talk and his hands constantly moved as he spoke. With all his charm, he should have been a salesman or teacher, not a bullwhacker loaned out to a turkey drive.

At first I thought he was a young man, even though fine wrinkles creased his face around his eyes. His hair was jet black, shiny as could be, and his skin a rich deep brown. He was the most handsome man I had ever seen. I was shocked when he told me he had a son that would be getting married at Christmas time.

"When we get to Rapid City, we'll have a little fun with the man who runs the mercantile there. We'll pretend Bill is our boss. I'll speak only Spanish and you act like you don't understand nothing."

"That's a bad idea. Mr. Peach won't like it," I said.

"Oh, c'mon. We'll have a big laugh together." He slapped my shoulder lightly and urged his horse into an easy lope.

Bill had been sitting next to us, staring out there. Maybe at the fringe of mountains on the horizon or maybe at the clouds. It was hard to tell. I didn't want any part of making him the butt of a joke. If Rufus ever found out, he'd probably whip us.

Pine-covered hills rose around us as we descended into the valley of Rapid Creek. We were at the very edge of the mountains. We stopped outside the settlement and Mr. Mendez promised me no one would be worse off for the trick he planned to play on the storekeeper. Reluctantly, I agreed to go along. We put our supply list in the pocket of Bill's old army blouse and rode into town and up to the mercantile.

Mr. Mendez pushed Bill along in front of him.

"Good morning, gentlemen!" the storekeeper said loudly. He wore a bit of a frown, a black hat, and a dirty white apron. "What are your needs?"

Mr. Mendez said something in Spanish.

"What was that?"

Mr. Mendez said the same thing again, only louder. Almost instantly, the storekeeper pulled a sawed-off shotgun from under the counter, pointed it at Mr. Mendez's chest, scolded him roundly and ordered him out of the store. All in perfect Spanish. At least I think that's what it was.

His hands raised, Mr. Mendez backed out of the store, totally surprised.

"So what in tarnation is this?" the merchant growled at me.

I explained that we were trailing a herd to Deadwood and had to replace supplies ruined by rain a few days earlier.

"You with that crazy turkey herd?" he boomed.

"Yessir. With Rufus Peach and a whole crew."

"So they say. I've known Bill here for almost a year. That Mendez fella don't remember me, but we been through this routine before a few years back in south Texas. He's a real joker."

I told him we needed the goods delivered.

"Yes, yes, Mendez already told me that. Besides, I want

a look at those birds you have. I'll be out this afternoon."

Bill and I walked back out into the sunlight and wind. Mr. Mendez as sitting on his horse, waiting patiently. The fact that his prank had failed had no effect at all on him.

I had heard that teamsters and bullwhackers were great practical jokers, playing tricks on each other often, trying to outdo each other. After this, I hoped Mr. Mendez would not try again soon. That, of course, was not to be.

As we rode back from Rapid City, I had the gnawing feeling that we were being watched. As far as I knew, only Bill was carrying a pistol. If road agents or an Indian war party came after us, we'd be at their mercy. On the other hand, we were watching for trouble and had good mounts in case we had to run for it.

Then I remembered that we had bought no socks while in Rapid City. I yelled this information to Mr. Mendez. He just laughed and kept riding for camp.

The wind howled and snapped at us all day. As promised, the merchant brought our food staples in the back of a buckboard. All afternoon, spectators rode out to our camp to see the flock of turkeys and the soft-headed bunch of drovers that had trailed them from Fort Pierre.

That night the wind calmed down some, but kept blowing till morning, whipping the canvas cover on the small wagon. For a long time, the racket kept me awake. Again, I worried about not finding Lucinda in the gold camp of Deadwood. *What if she's gone back east again?* That upset me for a while. But I knew I would have money in my pockets again at the end of the drive. If she were no longer there, I could take the stagecoach back to Fort Pierre. I'd track her down, no matter how far away she had wandered.

The next day was warmer and sunny. The turkeys dawdled along, but the nice weather made their pokiness tolerable. I was still walking behind the flock while all the other drovers rode their horses. Bill was in good spirits, sitting his mule as proudly as Gen. Ulysses S. Grant. He was circling the herd again, happy not to have any other riders interfering. Rufus was also in high spirits, whistling a merry tune between bursts of cussing at the bulls.

At the morning break, Mr. Mendez rode up with one of the grain sacks in his hand. Something heavy was inside.

"Heh, heh, heh." Mr. Mendez couldn't keep from laughing. "A leetle bedtime surprise for *el Rufus*," he whispered to me. He made sure the string around the opening was tied tight. Without asking me whether I minded, he put it inside the small wagon.

What was in the bag? Buffalo chips? Some kind of animal? A clump of prickly pear?

"What *is* that?" I asked suspiciously. Whatever he was hiding in the small wagon was in *my* sleeping area and I didn't want to be any part of any silly prank.

"You'll see!" he replied, adding another "Heh, heh, heh."

The afternoon passed without anything special happening. We let the turkeys and bulls forage for a while, set up the wire pen, and made ready to camp for the night. Besides the Black Hills rising to the south and west of us, the tip of another mountain peeped over the horizon to the northwest. I was curious about it, but decided to wait until we got closer before asking about it.

The sight seers were beginning to get on my nerves

now. They always laughed at us, asked "Did you ever see such a sight?" or "Can you believe that?" and made other dumb remarks. A few people offered to buy a bird or two, but Rufus turned them down flat.

While cooking supper, I noticed that the sack Mr. Mendez had hidden in the small wagon was gone. I asked him if he had moved it.

"No, no, Joshua. I'll do that after dark."

"But Luis, *it's gone.* It's not there anymore!"

"Not there?" He put his hand to his mouth. "Oh, my goo'ness!"

His being disturbed alarmed me instantly. *"What on earth was in that sack?"* I demanded.

"Eet was a beeg snake," he said with an impish grin. "He was sunning himself when I caught heem."

That made my skin crawl. Right away, I climbed up into the wagon to make sure the beast was really gone. I shook out all the blankets and my buffalo robe to make sure. No doubt this was another Mendez practical joke that was going to backfire.

Chapter 17
Gratitude

The weather grew gloomy and cold during the next four days. The solitary mountain to the northwest, called Bear Butte, rose as we got closer. Mr. Mendez said that it was a sacred place to the Cheyenne Indians, like Mount Sinai in the Bible.

I kept waiting for the missing snake to turn up in Rufus's bedroll, but it didn't. Meanwhile, Mr. Mendez put a big spoonful of salt in the boss's bean soup one night. Rufus got even by hiding the joker's boots so he had to ride in stocking feet all the next day. Playing tricks on each other was something they enjoyed without really getting mad when victimized. But the missing snake bothered me. Maybe it had escaped and crawled back into the ground before the cold weather arrived. But that wasn't very likely.

An occasional flake of snow wafted down the morning we started out just south of Bear Butte. By mid-morning, it was snowing so hard we couldn't see a quarter of a mile. The birds' feet were cold and they sometimes stopped to lift one foot up into their feathers to warm it before moving on. Traveling in such bad weather seemed cruel to the turkeys and hard on us drovers, too.

But Rufus insisted on pressing on. At midmorning, there was no foraging for the bulls or the turkeys because three inches of heavy, wet snow covered the ground. By noon—when we usually set off for another two or three hours of driving—the snowstorm had worsened so we could see only a hundred feet or so. Rufus told us to put up the wire pen and get the turkeys inside. He kept hoping out loud that the storm would stop soon so we could move on, but snow continued to fall heavily in a stiff wind. Sometime before dawn, it quit and the sky cleared.

In some places, the snow had drifted three feet deep. In other spots, there was practically none, having blown away. The cold and snowdrifts in some places made it hard to roll out in the morning. I got out my heavy mittens and wished I had oiled boots to keep my feet dry walking in the snow.

By late afternoon, we got to Crook City—named for the Army's General George C. Crook, not bandits—which Rufus said was the last settlement before Deadwood. There were a few shanties thrown up with crudely sawed wooden slabs and a couple of log cabins, but most of the village consisted of tents. The U.S. Cavalry had a detachment camped there to protect the gold miners from hostile Indians. There was an air of excitement about the place, lots of talk about the latest gold strikes and new places to dig. The idea of looking for gold in the snow and ice did not excite me.

And, as always, the gawkers were coming out to see us like flies attracted to fresh meat. By now we were all weary of jokes about turkeys, turkey feathers, people trying to mimic a gobbler, and asking if we'd "talk turkey" about selling them a bird.

In full daylight, a man with a heavy gray beard climbed into the pen, caught a bird, and tried to carry it off. When Rufus saw the thief trying to get out of the pen, he gave him a blistering blast of verbal fire and warned him that he would be shot if he came back.

Now many spectators were coming from Deadwood, only a few miles up in the mountains. Time and again, I asked if they knew my sister, Lucinda Greene. No one had ever heard of her. By that night, my stomach ached from fear that I wouldn't find her.

With so much snow on the ground and likely trouble driving the turkeys through the forest, Rufus said he would haul a load or two in his tandem wagon and hire other wagoneers to take the rest of the birds to the mining camp. So, he paid off the Bostonians, Messrs. Brady and Forbes, and thanked them for their help. He also paid off the teamsters from Mr. Volin's wagon train, Messrs. Mendez and Olson. They took their money gratefully, but said they'd stay with the flock until sold so they'd get back the money owed their friends. Rufus wasn't pleased to hear this, but he really didn't have any choice.

I expected the boss to pay me off next and send me on my way, too. Instead, he started waddling off toward the big wagon.

"What about me?" I yelled desperately.

"What about you?" Rufus grumbled.

"You won't be needing me any longer. I mean, we're practically in Deadwood, and—"

"Hold on a minute! It's gonna take us two more days at least to get them birds to Deadwood. Someone has to look after them. Someone has to keep our camp going. Someone has to cook."

"But Mr. Mendez can cook."

"Harrumph! He'd poison me if he got a chance!"

"So when will I be through?"

"When we're done." With that, he stomped off to his wagon.

So now I was Rufus Peach's slave, being held against my wishes, kept from finding my sister. It felt worse than being stuck on Uncle Asa's hog farm back in Illinois.

While cooking supper, Mr. Mendez and I had to chase away two more men trying to help themselves to our turkeys. I still liked Luis very much. He was so charming and fun to be around. For a while I had thought about telling him about my search for my sister, but I was afraid he'd turn that into a prank; maybe tell her that I was lost in the mountains or something ridiculous like that.

We were wiping the tin plates when Bill trudged over in the snow. I handed him a dish towel, draping it over his forearm, like a butler. For a while he stared off into the night. But then, after seeing what Mr. Mendez and I were doing, he picked up the last plate, wiped it on the inside and put it away. After weeks of encouraging him to help, he finally wiped one plate!

We had a nice big campfire going to keep us warm until we turned in. I was thinking about the letters I had to write to Aunt Clara and to the Doaks family about the fate of the Three Fugitives.

This trip has certainly taken its toll. Gone forever are Zebulon Smith, Joe Doaks, Joe Jones, Joe Black, Stonewall Sharps, and at least ten road agents, as well as two or three dozen turkeys. And the buffalo hunters, Messrs. Winchester, Colt, and Springfield, are probably on their way to prison.

When I arrived in Yankton, I was afraid of everyone, but now I knew I could survive real danger. I could earn my living. Why, I had even stood up to the likes of Rufus Peach. For sure, I was no longer a rank greenhorn. That made me feel proud.

Rufus came with his tin cup, poured some coffee, added a splash of whiskey from a small bottle in his coat and sat down beside me.

"Well, Josh, when I first seen you, I asked myself, 'What rock did that worm crawl out from under?' You turned out a whole load better than them others. Look at all the quitters we had. Them cowpunchers, that bony old trapper and his Injuns, them convicts, and them buffalo hunters." He stopped to slurp some of his coffee.

"We couldn't of made it without you. You can cook good, too."

This kind of talk made me wonder how much liquor he had had already. His tongue was well oiled and he was in a warm, pleasant mood, a rare thing for Rufus Peach.

"You and me agreed on a dollar a day," he drawled on. "But as a well-earned thank-you, I'll be payin' you two dollars a day. That's a total of a hundred dollars—three, four months wages for most men."

I was shocked, but thanked him heartily.

"My advice now," Rufus said, looking me in the eye, "is take some of that money and buy yourself a horse. You done enough walkin' for a lifetime on this trip."

"Yessir." For once, Rufus had made me feel so good that I unexpectedly said, "I'm glad we did this together. It's a trip I'll always treasure."

He slapped my back and went back to his wagon, muttering that tomorrow would be a long day.

Messrs. Mendez and Olson were sitting by the fire, dozing in its light and warmth. I told them that someone needed to keep a watch for prowlers. They said they'd keep a lookout.

I lit a candle from the fire and went back to the small wagon to re-arrange the contents of my valise. Near the bottom I found the letter from Saint Louis addressed to Lucinda the postmaster in Kankakee had given me. I suspected it was from her beau, Malcolm. *If I don't find you in Deadwood, I'm going to open that letter to know for sure and to pay you back for being so hard to find.*

At breakfast the next morning, Mr. Mendez was shoveling biscuits and gravy into his mouth faster than I'd ever seen before. Rufus walked up and said, "Luis! I think this is yours." He handed the teamster a long stick that was pointed at one end.

Mr. Mendez took hold of it without actually looking first. When he saw what he had, he jumped up, spilled the remaining biscuits and gravy on his pants and let out a yowl. Then he dropped the stick. Rufus had handed him the snake that had been missing for a week. In the cold weather, it had become rigid.

The boss and Mr. Olson howled with laughter until tears ran down their cheeks. Bill gave them a sour look and walked away. The joke was funny all right, but not *that* funny.

That morning we loaded the wagons with turkeys that Rufus would take to Deadwood. Our job was to guard the remaining birds and supplies. He said he'd be back the next day. As I watched him leave, I knew the wait would be torture for me.

Chapter 18
Deadwood

Having all the firewood you want is a wonderful thing. For nearly fifty days, I had often tried to cook with handfuls of twigs, twisted grass, and dried buffalo chips for lack of wood. Luckily, Rufus's kitchen included a small stove that burned kerosene, which we used when we found no other fuel.

But now we were in the Black Hills, covered with great pine trees, spruce, birch, and even some cottonwoods. Almost everywhere you looked, there was wood to be cut for the fire. Messrs. Mendez and Olson had time on their hands. Rather than sit idle, they spent the next day cutting wood so we had a roaring fire all day. The weather had become milder so that snow melted in the sunlight, but lingered in the shade under trees and near buildings.

I had packed and repacked my valise a half-dozen times, waiting for tomorrow. After finishing, I'd get to wondering about my socks, or a set of long-john underwear or some other silly thing and have to open the latches and dig inside to know for sure.

A steady stream of sightseers continued to come to see the turkeys, including a group of Chinese workers from the mining camp. Some of the curiosity-seekers looked pitifully poor and hungry. Others acted suspicious, so Bill and I were on guard all day, our pistols showing, to make sure no one helped himself to a gobbler.

One young man and his older partner inspected the birds carefully and said they wanted to buy some for breeding stock.

"You'll have to ask the owner," I replied. I was almost afraid to ask, but I had to. "Are there any bakeries in Deadwood?"

"Bakeries?" the younger man asked.

"Yeah, you know, where they make bread, pies, pastries. Good stuff like that."

"Oh, sure. There's three or four. There *was* one run by two young women, but I noticed yesterday it was closed. I guess Deadwood was too rough a place for them."

Now I was sorry I had asked. And I knew the only way I'd learn whether Lucinda was in the gold camp was to go find her myself. But I couldn't do that before tomorrow.

Late in the afternoon, Rufus returned to camp, smiling and humming happily. I suspected he had been drinking again, but stayed far away enough not to smell his breath.

"Sold the whole load!" he bragged. "It was so easy I couldn't believe it. Must have taken in a thousand dollars."

Messrs. Mendez and Olson would have been glad to hear that, but they were still up on a hillside cutting wood.

"I went looking for your sister," Rufus said with a roguish look on his face. "But when I tried to ask about her, I realized I didn't know her name and I had no idea where to look for her. In fact, I don't even know *your* full name."

"That's all right," I said. Wild horses couldn't have dragged that out of me now. Rufus Peach would just have to live out his life without knowing my sister's name or anything else about her.

He said that in the morning six wagons would come for the rest of the turkeys. Still, he didn't offer to pay me off. I guess he knew that if he gave me my wages, I'd be gone like a wisp of smoke in the mountain air.

In the late afternoon, we fed the turkeys and the bulls as the sun was dipping into the horizon. Carrying pails of grain for the birds had become a habit for me and other members of the crew. I guessed that this would be the last time I did that job. In a way I was so happy to end this journey, but knowing it was over brought a little sadness, too.

As night fell, we built up the fire again and Mr. Mendez and I started supper. Rufus brought us a big ham and a batch of potatoes, which we fried. We also baked cornbread in the Dutch oven.

Rufus talked and talked at supper, telling of all the people he had seen in Deadwood, recalling their comments about the turkeys. It made me feel good to see him sounding so happy. In fact, his good mood had all of us feeling excited about getting to the gold camp.

Except for Bill. As always, he had that far-away look, but now there seemed to be a shadow of sadness in his blank eyes. I tried to talk to him , but soon gave it up.

When we were done eating, Rufus invited Messrs. Mendez and Olson to take a stroll with him down to the noisier end of the main street of Crook City. I figured they were going to a saloon. Perhaps Rufus would taunt them into playing poker and he'd win their earnings back. I guessed he played better than anyone suspected. Everyone said if he won a little, he was lucky; if he won a lot, he cheated. My hunch was that he played poker with great skill.

When the three left, they said they'd be back in an hour and would stand night guard from then on. But for now, they said to watch for thieves. I told them we had everything under control.

As I washed the tin plates and pans, I remembered the times Zebulon Smith had helped me, spinning his tales of the early days in beaver country, what he loved to call "shinin' times." Back in the shadows, with flickering flames lighting their faces, John Blood and Eagle Screams would listen, nodding now and then, and speak softly in Crow. "By now, John Blood and Eagle must be back with their people in the Bighorns," I murmured to myself.

Bill gave me a quizzical look, as if to ask, "What's wrong with you, boy?"

I explained to him what I had been thinking about.

"We're a long way from home, Bill. But, you know, we took good care of each other and that got us through."

Because there were so few dishes to dry, I did them all myself while Bill stood by, gazing at the fire for a while, then looking out over the turkey pen. I could hear a couple of dogs barking at the other end of the little town, the faint tinkle of a piano in a bar and the din of men talking loud there, too.

"Bill, there probably won't be a good time to say goodbye tomorrow, what with loading the turkeys and all. So I want to say goodbye to you tonight."

Again, he looked into my eyes.

"I'll always remember you and this trip. Catching you taking a bath in that little puddle of water off the trail will always make me laugh! Bill, I wish you well."

I reached out to shake his hand. Remembering how I never really said goodbye to Zebulon Smith or to Father or to Mother, I had a sudden urge to give Bill a hug. My wrapping my arms around him must have surprised him, because after a second, he pulled away. I was amazed at how thin and bony that old soldier was.

His eyes met mine again for an instant. Then, in total silence, he mouthed the words "Thank you." A second later, his eyes were hazy again. He turned and walked to the far side of the turkey pen to keep watch until Rufus and the others came back.

It was still dark when the freight wagons from Deadwood arrived in the morning. We made breakfast for our men and the teamsters and were scrambling to catch the gangling turkeys and load them just after daybreak. The sun was just rising on the snowy November morning as we pulled out of Crook City for Deadwood. The trip was up, up into the mountains, beautifully wooded with ample snow on the ground. I was glad Rufus had chosen not to try to drive the birds on this road. We could never have kept them out of the trees.

As always, Rufus took the lead with his team of bulls.

The other wagons had teams of mules or horses, able to go much faster than the oxen, which made the drivers complain loudly. But they stayed in line behind the boss.

Coming into Deadwood Gulch brought us down a steep, narrow road into the gold camp at midday. The muddy streets were full of people, wagons, horses, mules, and bull teams. When the men there saw the wagonloads of turkeys, they cheered and clapped their hands, whistled and hooted with excitement. We set up the wire pen for one last time and put the big birds inside it.

Several large, loud men were slapping Rufus on the back, telling him what a grand job he had done with the turkeys. Others were standing around, waiting for a chance to buy one of the birds.

"I believe that wraps up the drive," I said to the boss.

"Yes, sir. We did it." Rufus pulled a leather bag out of his pocket and took out five twenty-dollar gold pieces. "Here you go. Thanks for your help."

"Thank you. Now, I owe you a dollar drawn in advance."

"Keep it. You earned it. Take a turkey, too."

"No thanks, I've had all the turkey I want for a while. As soon as I find my sister, I'll be back for my things."

He nodded. Someone was pulling at his sleeve to buy a turkey.

That's when I started up the street, looking for Lucinda. I had gone two blocks when I found a storefront that had a small "Bakery" sign dangling lopsidedly on one hook. Now the building was empty and closed. Out of curiosity, I cupped my hands over my eyes and looked inside through the dirty glass. There was no way of knowing who had run this business, but I had a horrible feeling it had been my sister. *I'm too late again.*

A hopeless feeling came over me. A lump rose in my throat and my eyes began to burn. I was afraid I was going to start crying. With all the people around, that was the last thing I wanted to do. I leaned against the glass, keeping my hands up to hide my face.

I could hear two women clomping up the board walk toward me. They were merrily talking a mile a minute .

"Excuse me!" one of them called. "We've moved up the street two blocks. We'll be glad to serve you there."

It was Lucinda. I'd know her lilting voice anywhere. Slowly, I turned to face her.

Her mouth dropped open. Then she shrieked happily, "Joshua! You're finally here!" We flew into each others' arms for a huge hug. We both tried to speak at the same time. Finally I told her how I had gotten to Deadwood; she told me Mr. Langley, her partner's husband, had gotten well and arrived by stage coach only a week earlier. He brought news of seeing me in Pierre, but didn't know where I was, other than I had left for the Black Hills.

After talking for a little while, Lucinda gave me a funny look. "Josh, please don't take this the wrong way, *but you need a bath.* Then we can talk."

And so I took one. Afterwards, we talked and laughed and talked all night.

Historical Note

Before railroads and modern highways were common in the United States, farm animals were often driven on foot to market. The cattle drives from Texas to railroad shipping points in Kansas and Nebraska are well known. In those days, farmers and ranchers often trailed other kinds of livestock, too—horses, sheep, swine, and even poultry—long distances to market as occurs in *AFOOT*. This story was inspired by this brief historical account:

Turkey Drive

In the fall of 1878, two fearless and patient Volin brothers drove, like cattle, 1,200 turkeys from Fort Pierre to Deadwood, a cross-country distance of some 200 miles. They shipped the turkeys by boat from Yankton to Pierre, then hired wagons and helpers.

Although the turkeys weren't very cooperative, as no turkey is, they averaged five miles a day. The gobbling turkeys ate their way across the dangerous, grassy prairie, being kept in tow with grain and wild fruit found along the way. Each night the flock was herded into a wire mesh enclosure; crippled birds were carried in the wagons.

Having left Fort Pierre in late summer, they reached Deadwood just before Thanksgiving, selling all 1,200 turkeys to the miners for an average price of $15.00 apiece.
—*Cowboys and Sodbusters*, 1978.

This, of course wasn't the only turkey drive, nor the greatest. For example, in 1852, a man drove 2,000 turkeys from Independence, Missouri, to California, where he sold them at a huge profit.

Domesticated turkeys of the 1800s, unlike the plump, juicy birds now so popular for Thanksgiving dinner, were scrawny, long-legged, long-necked creatures. It was customary to clip their wing feathers to keep them from flying because they were so much like their wild cousins.

AFOOT is fiction. All of the characters, except for Mr. Volin, are completely imaginary. He is a combination of Louis and Joseph Volin, major freight wagon train operators on the Fort Pierre-Deadwood road and older brothers of the Volin boys who actually drove turkeys to Deadwood.

Kankakee, Illinois, Sioux City, Iowa, Yankton, Fort Pierre, Rapid City, Crook City (now a ghost town), and Deadwood existed in 1877. But the city of Pierre had not yet been settled as described in this story. It was laid out in 1878. Also, the steamboats *Key West* and *Nelly Peck* were among nearly forty vessels that plied the Missouri River that year. The riverboat *Sultana* exploded on the Mississippi River just thirteen days after the assassination of President Lincoln on April 14, 1865, killing at least 1,800 passengers.

Thousands of tons of freight, including food, tools, mining machinery, and even locomotives, were hauled by wagon to the Black Hills in the 1870s and later.

Travelers on the Fort Pierre-to-Deadwood road risked attack by Indians in 1876 and 1878, but no reported attacks took place during the period of this story. Robber's Roost was a notorious point near the trail crossing of the Cheyenne river. Because of the threat of raids by road agents, freighters usually avoided camping in the Cheyenne valley even though it offered firewood and water.

To better understand the trail and the country it crosses, the author bicycled 175 miles along its route. He also searched newspapers published in Deadwood and Yankton, Dakota Territory, for news of events of the time.

He is grateful to historians Herbert Hoover, Bob Lee, Watson Parker, James Volin, and Irma Klock for their help, to the Kankakee County Historical Society, to the International Steamboat Society for background information, to the South Dakota Historical Society for lending microfilm of Dakota Territory newspapers, and to anthropologist Martin Peterson and sociologist Karren Baird-Olson for sharing some of their knowledge of Native Americans. He also appreciates assistance from turkey grower Frank Reese, Jr.

Special thanks to the late Joan Lowery Nixon for her suggestions and encouragement on this project.

Give your friends and colleagues copies of the adventure story, *AFOOT*

Order it from your favorite book dealer or directly from the publisher, The Cedartip Company.

☐ **YES,** I want _____ hardcover copies of *AFOOT: a Tale of the Great Dakota Turkey Drive* for $22.80 each.

☐ **YES,** I want _____ paperback copies of *AFOOT: a Tale of the Great Dakota Turkey Drive* for $11.85 each.

Add $2.95 shipping and handling for one book, and $1.00 for each additional book. Kansas residents must include the applicable sales tax of 7.3 percent.

My check or money order for a total of $_____ is enclosed.

Please charge my ☐ VISA ☐ MasterCard

Name _____

Organization _____

Address _____

City/State/Zip _____

Phone _____ E-mail _____

Credit card no. _____

Expiration date _____

Signature _____

The Cedartip Company
P.O. Box 231
Manhattan, Kansas 66505-0231

Also, you can buy the book on-line at *www.cedartip.com*